MORE PRAISE FOR BABYMOUSE!

"Sassy, smart . . .
Babymouse is here
to stay."
—The Horn Book Magazine

"Young readers
will happily
fall in line."
—Kirkus Reviews

"The brother-sister creative team hits the mark
with humor, sweetness, and characters so genuine
they can pass for real kids." —Booklist

"Babymouse is spunky, ambitious,
and, at times, a total dweeb."
—School Library Journal

Be sure to read **all** the **BABYMOUSE** books:

#1 BABYMOUSE: Queen of the World!
#2 BABYMOUSE: Our Hero
#3 BABYMOUSE: Beach Babe
#4 BABYMOUSE: Rock Star
#5 BABYMOUSE: Heartbreaker
#6 CAMP BABYMOUSE
#7 BABYMOUSE: Skater Girl
#8 BABYMOUSE: Puppy Love
#9 BABYMOUSE: Monster Mash
#10 BABYMOUSE: The Musical
#11 BABYMOUSE: Dragonslayer
#12 BABYMOUSE: Burns Rubber

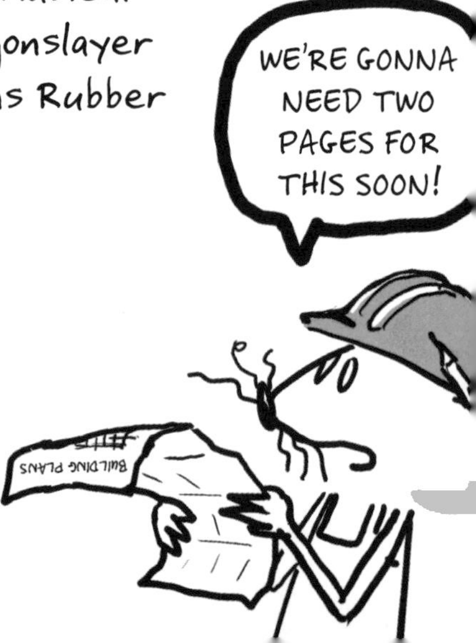
WE'RE GONNA NEED TWO PAGES FOR THIS SOON!
BUILDING PLANS

BABYMOUSE
BURNS RUBBER

BY JENNIFER L. HOLM & MATTHEW HOLM

RANDOM HOUSE NEW YORK

I'M MAKING A PIT STOP.

Copyright © 2010 by Jennifer Holm and Matthew Holm

All rights reserved.
Published in the United States by Random House Children's Books,
a division of Random House, Inc., New York.

Random House and the colophon are registered trademarks of Random House, Inc.

Visit us on the Web! www.randomhouse.com/kids
www.babymouse.com

Educators and librarians, for a variety of teaching tools,
visit us at www.randomhouse.com/teachers

Library of Congress Cataloging-in-Publication Data
Holm, Jennifer L.
Babymouse : burns rubber / by Jennifer and Matthew Holm. — 1st ed.
   p. cm.
Summary: Babymouse's dreams of being a race car driver come true when she and
her best friend Wilson enter a soap box derby.
ISBN 978-0-375-85713-3 (trade pbk.) — ISBN 978-0-375-95713-0 (lib. bdg.)
[1. Graphic novels. [1. Graphic novels. 2. Imagination—Fiction. 3. Soap box derbies—Fiction.
4. Mice—Fiction. 5. Animals—Fiction. 6. Humorous stories.]
I. Holm, Matthew. II. Title. III. Title: Burns rubber.
PZ7.7.H65Bad 2010 741.5'973—dc22 2009018819

MANUFACTURED IN MALAYSIA   10 9 8 7 6   First Edition

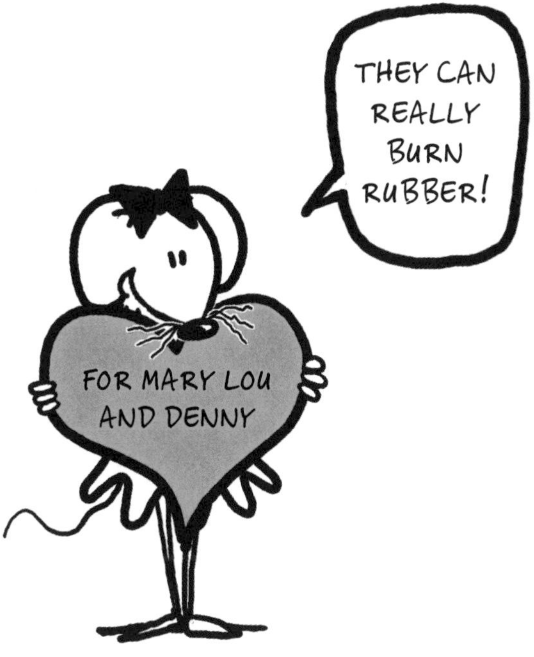
THEY CAN REALLY BURN RUBBER!
FOR MARY LOU AND DENNY

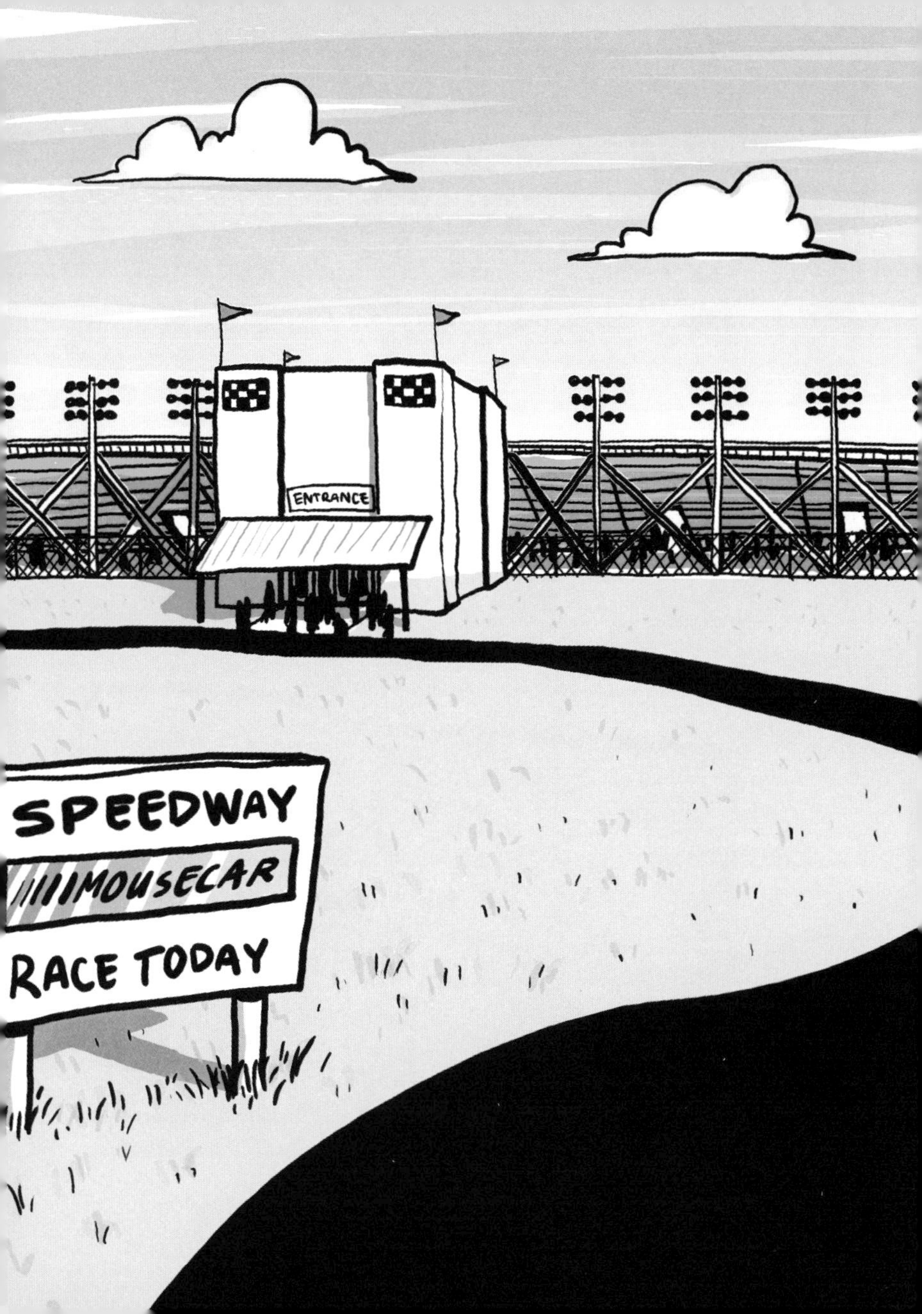
ENTRANCE
SPEEDWAY
MOUSECAR
RACE TODAY

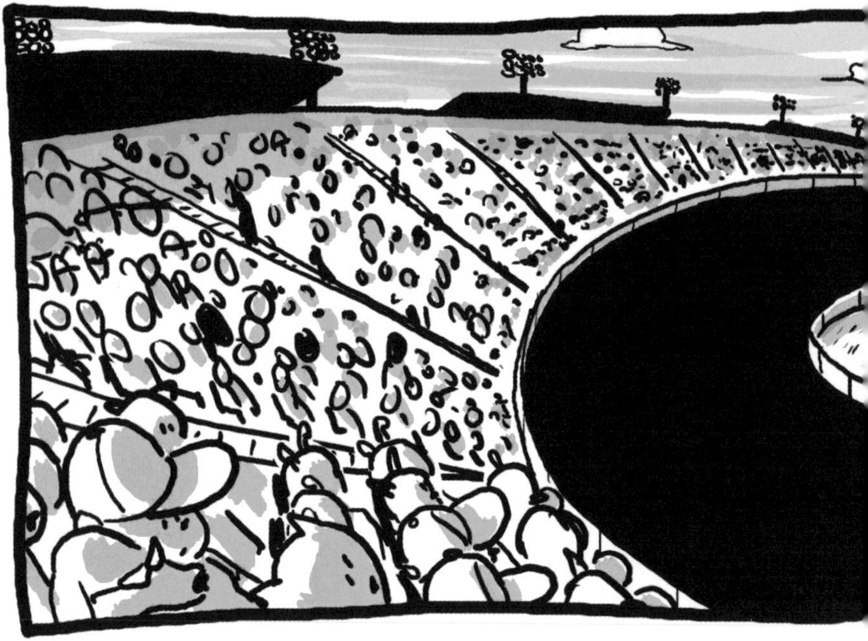

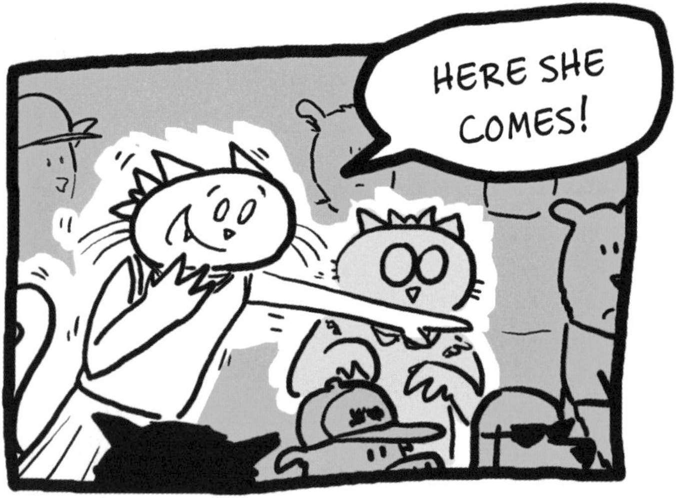
HERE SHE COMES!

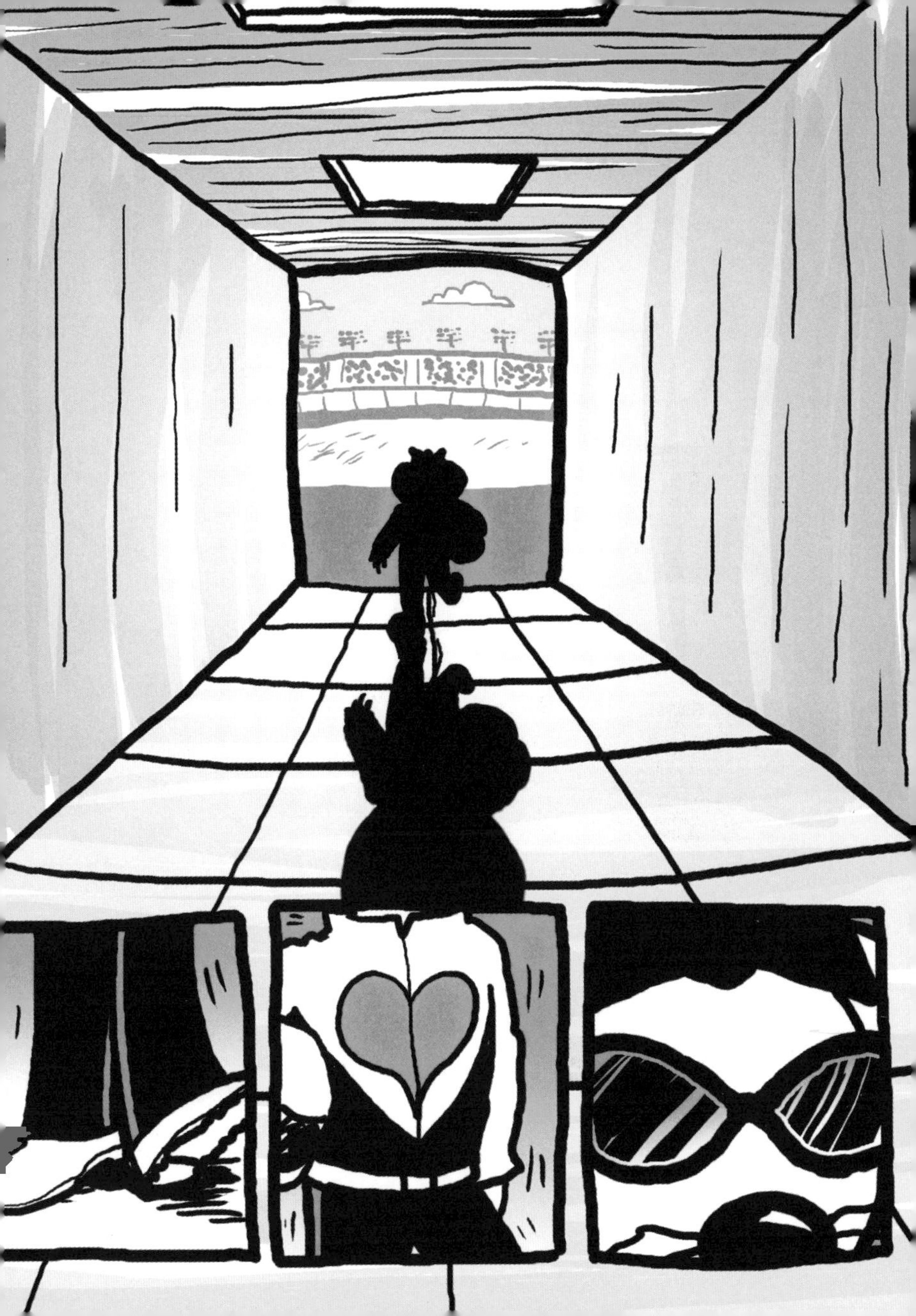

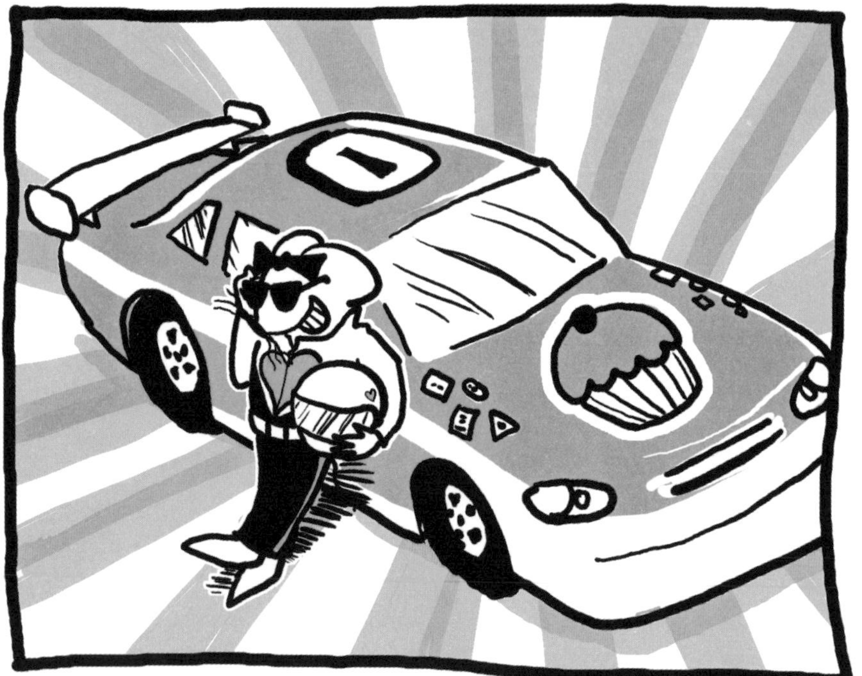

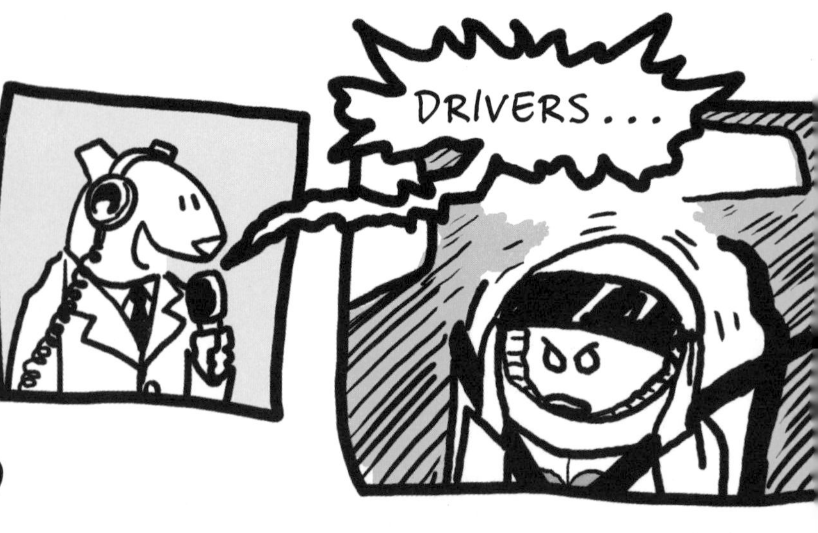
DRIVERS ...

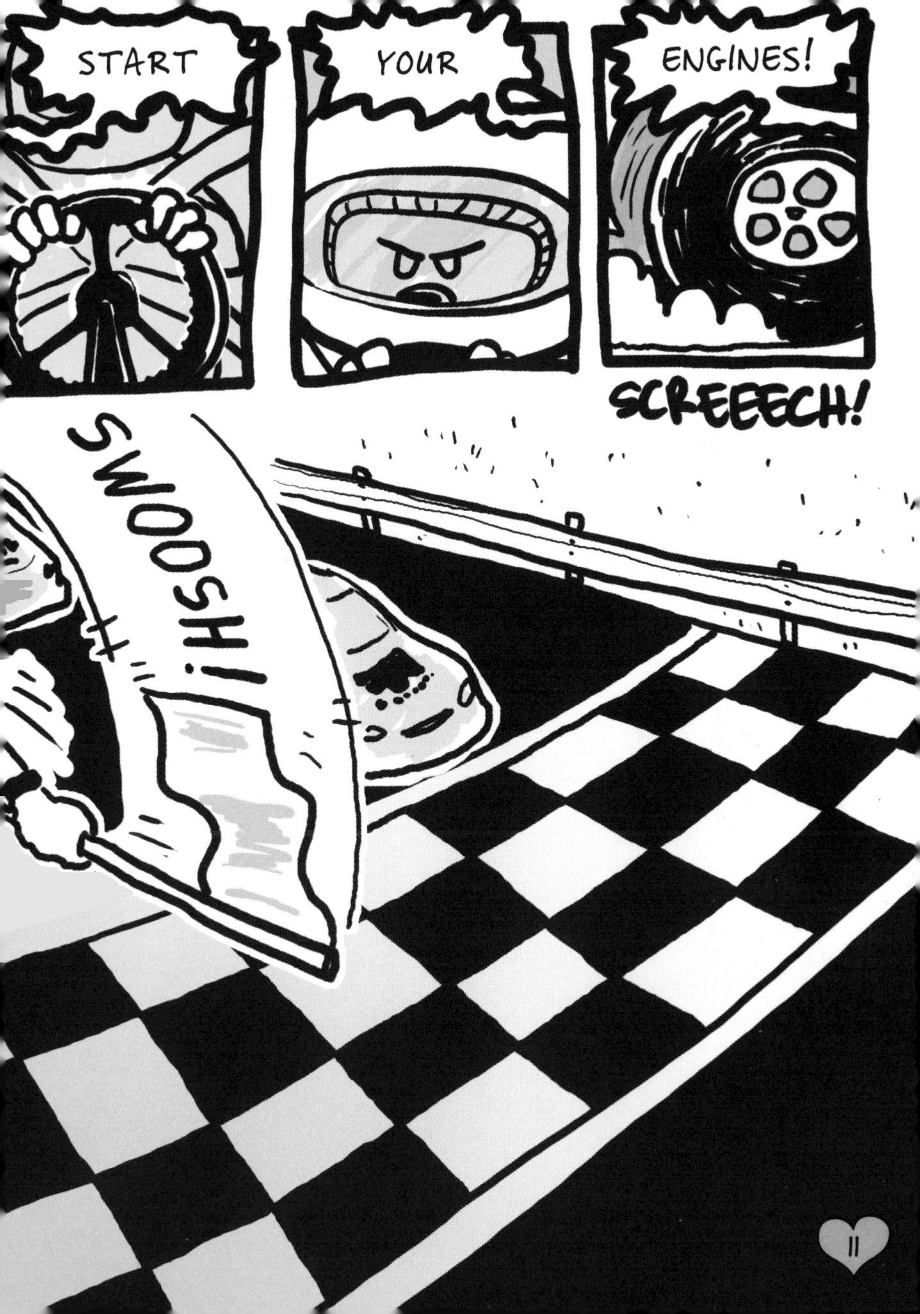
START
YOUR
ENGINES!
SCREEECH!
SWOOSH!

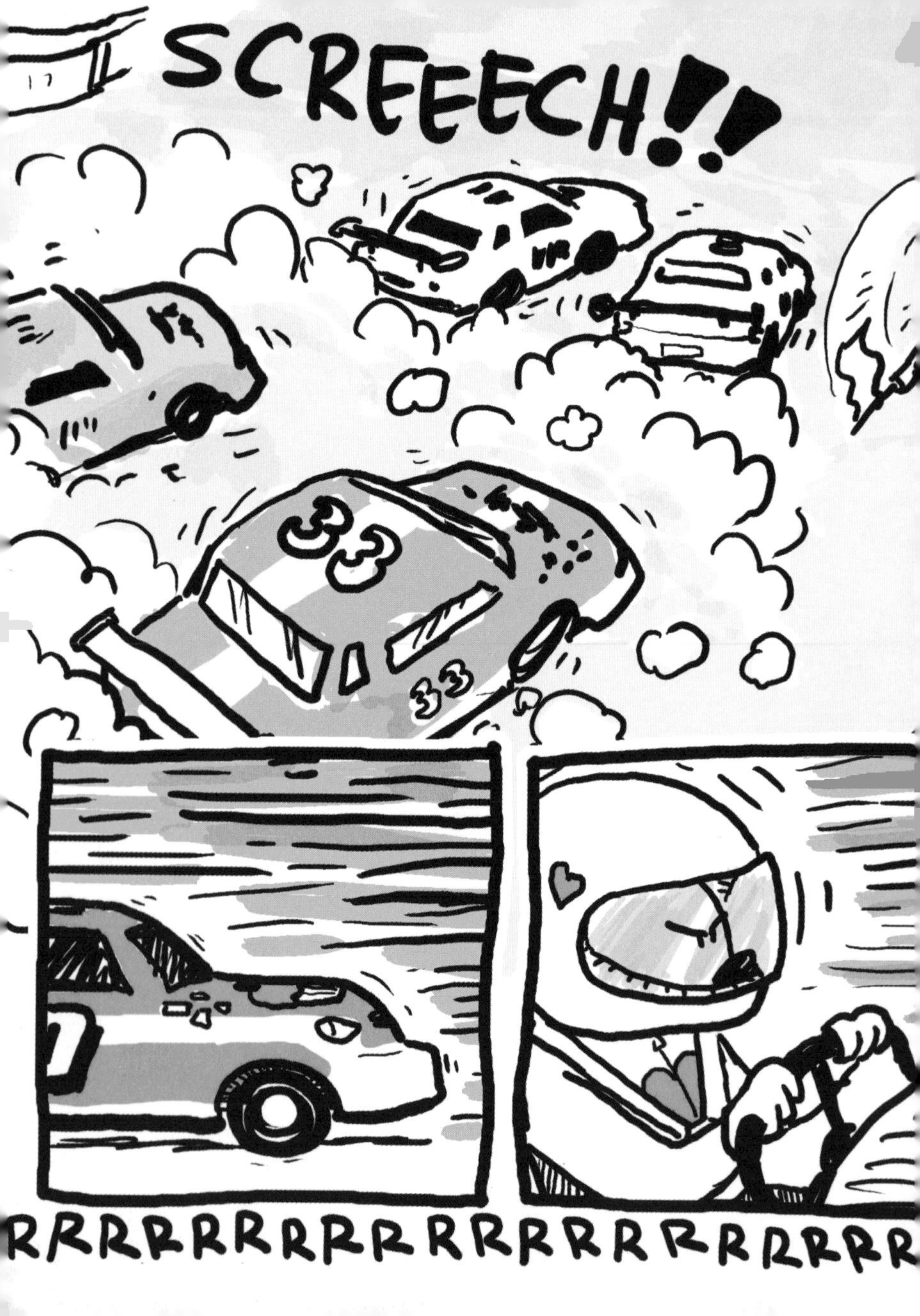
SCREEECH!!!
33
33
RRRRRRRRRRRRRRRRRRRR

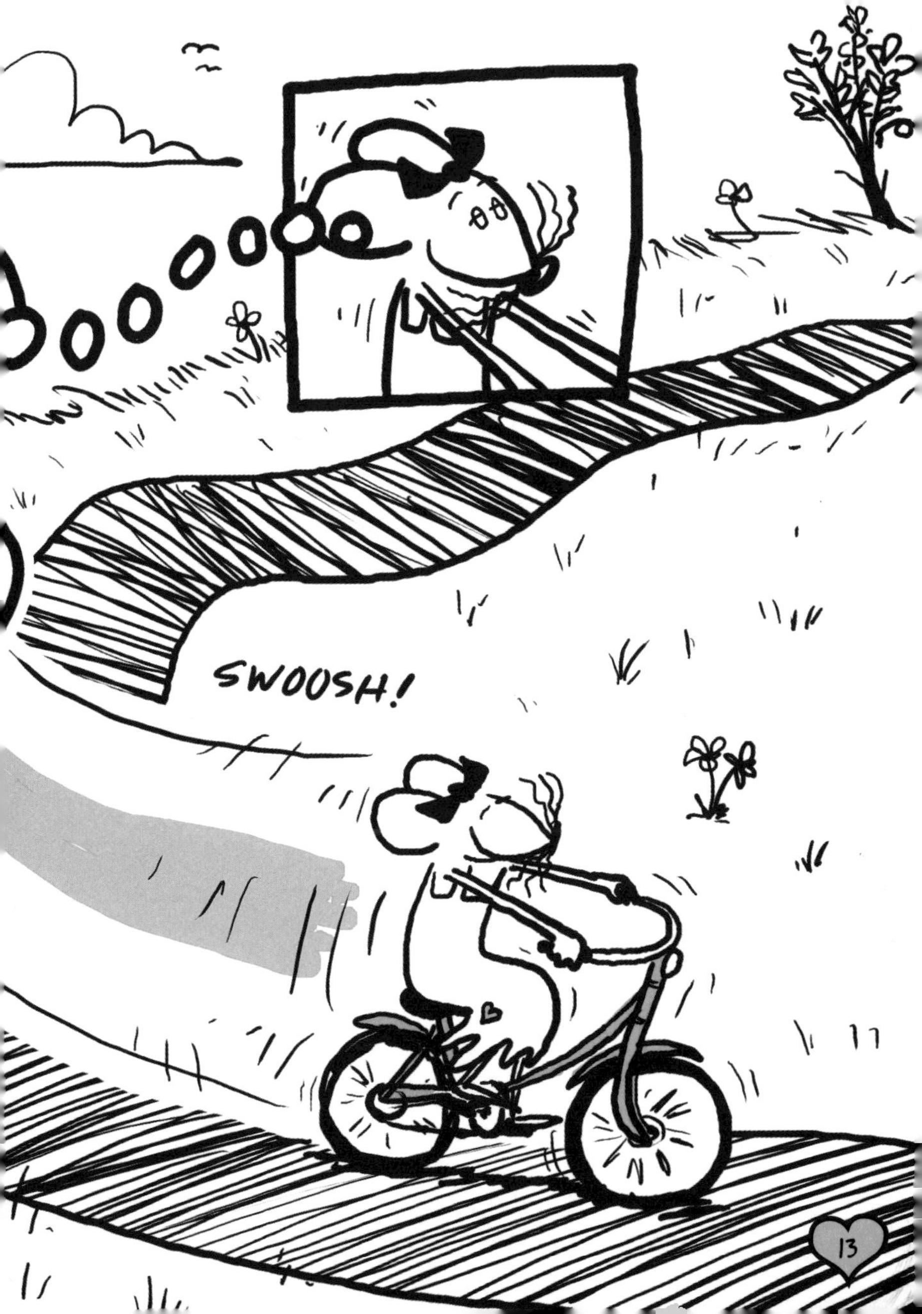
SWOOSH!

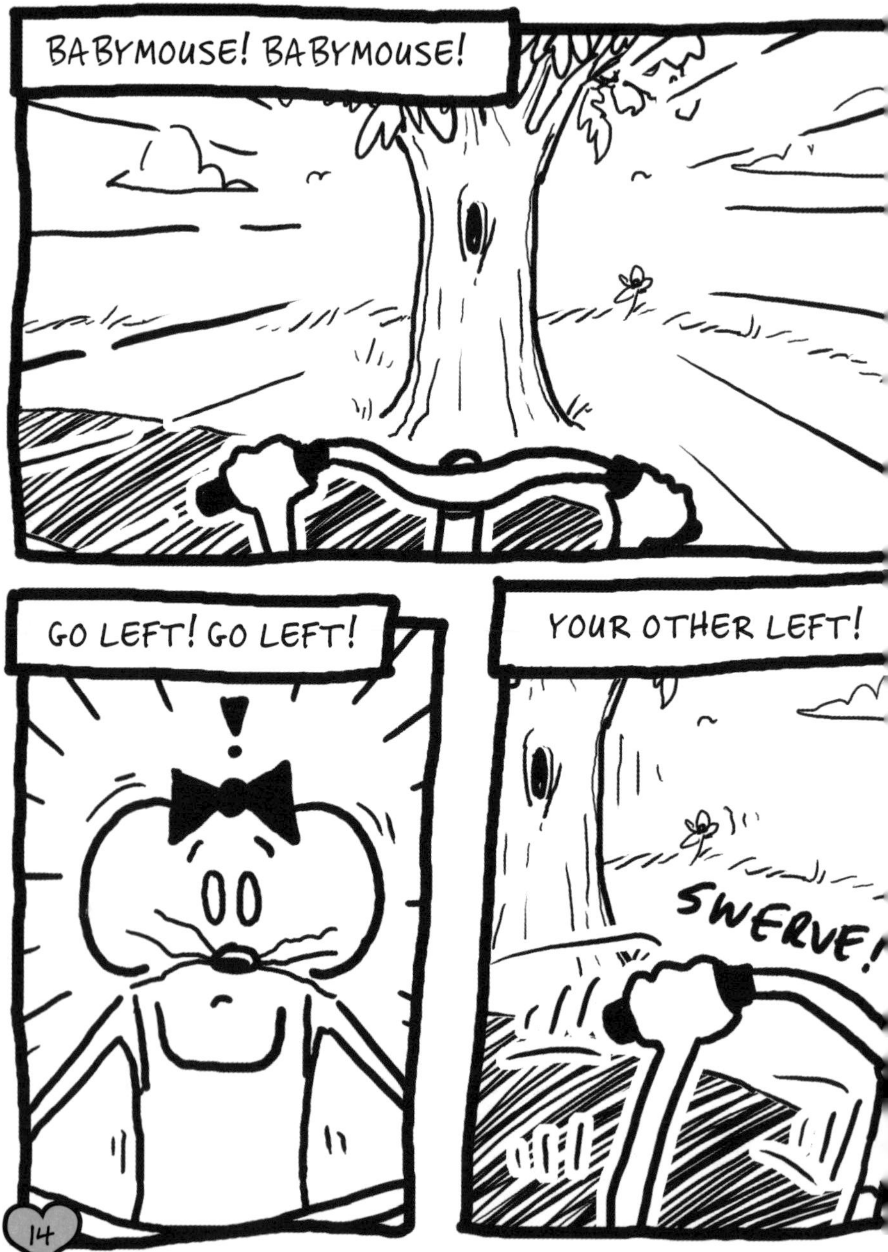
BABYMOUSE! BABYMOUSE!
GO LEFT! GO LEFT!
!
YOUR OTHER LEFT!
SWERVE!

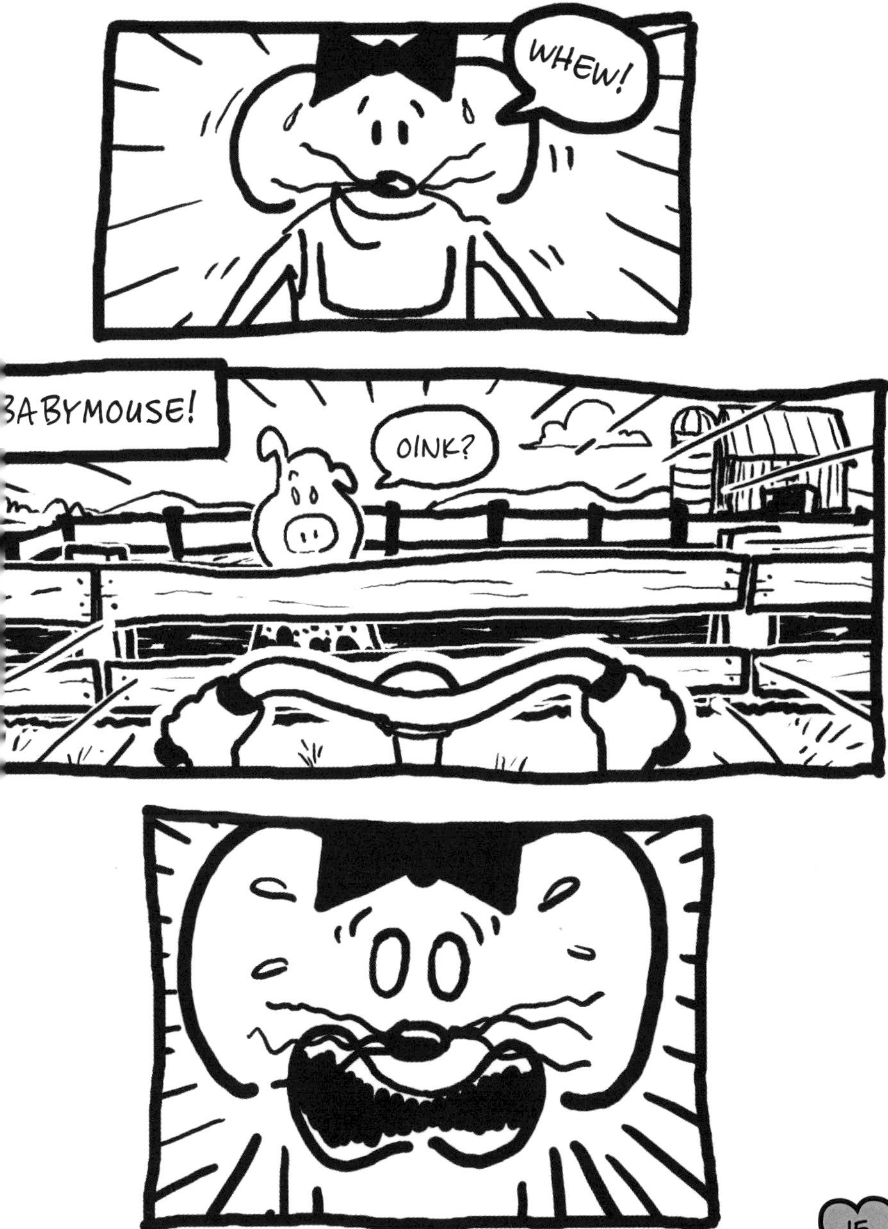
WHEW!
BABYMOUSE!
OINK?

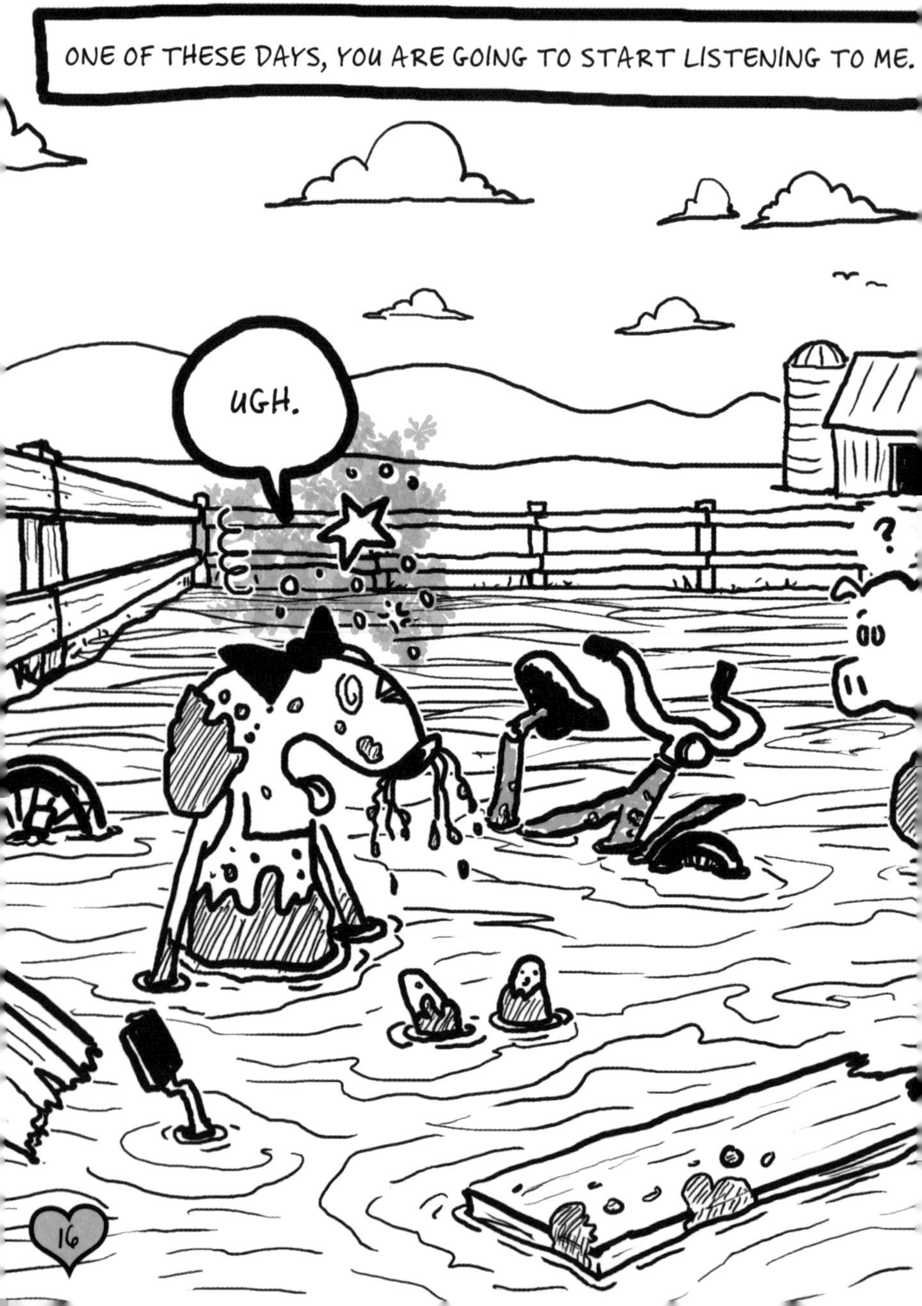
ONE OF THESE DAYS, YOU ARE GOING TO START LISTENING TO ME.
UGH.
?

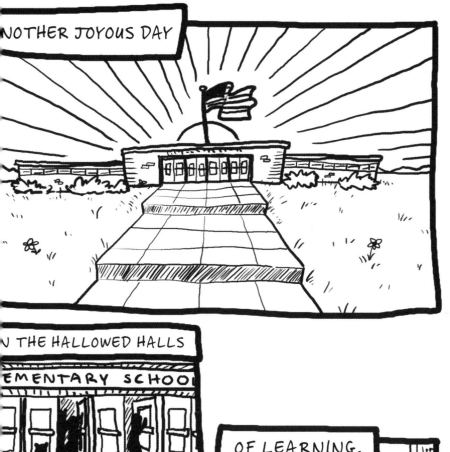

ANOTHER JOYOUS DAY

IN THE HALLOWED HALLS

EMENTARY SCHOO

OF LEARNING.

17

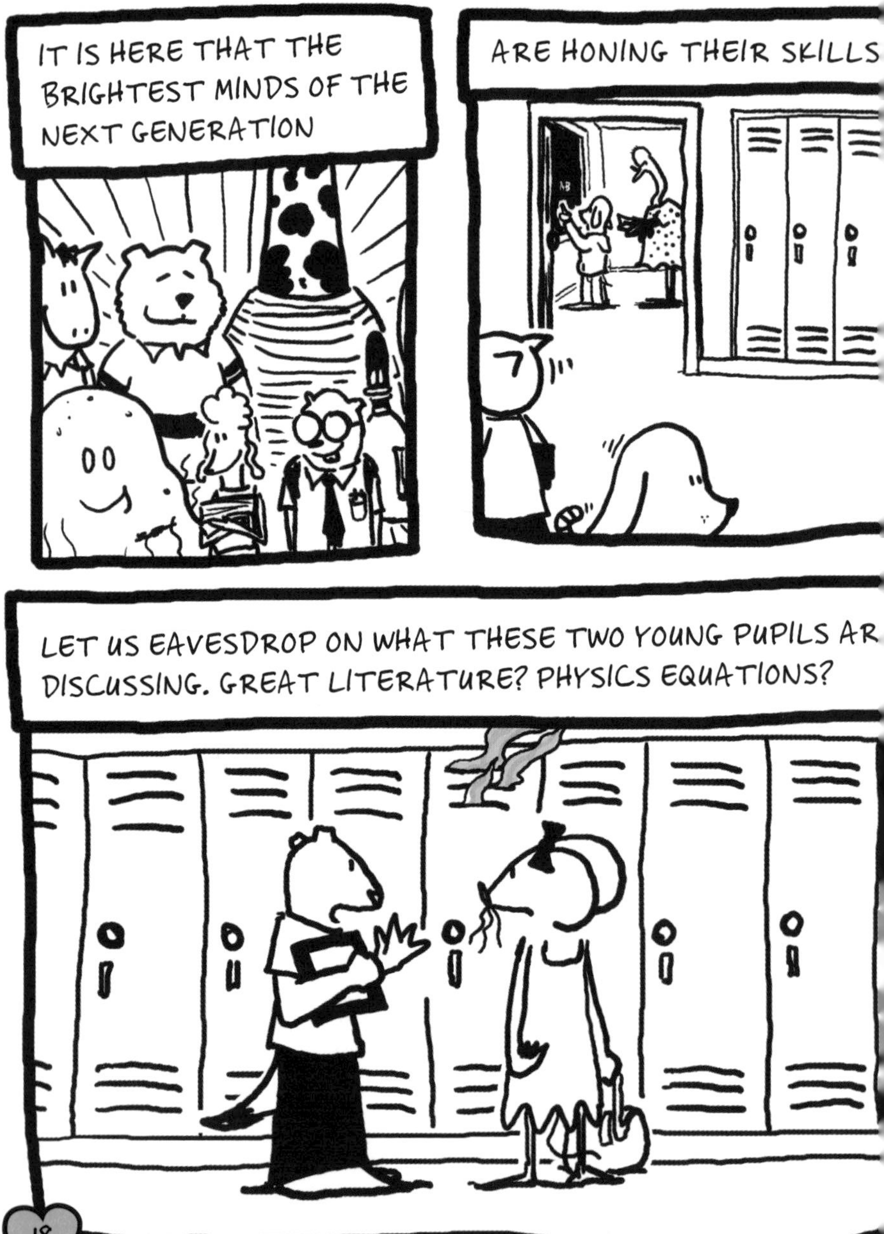
IT IS HERE THAT THE BRIGHTEST MINDS OF THE NEXT GENERATION
ARE HONING THEIR SKILLS
LET US EAVESDROP ON WHAT THESE TWO YOUNG PUPILS AR
DISCUSSING. GREAT LITERATURE? PHYSICS EQUATIONS?

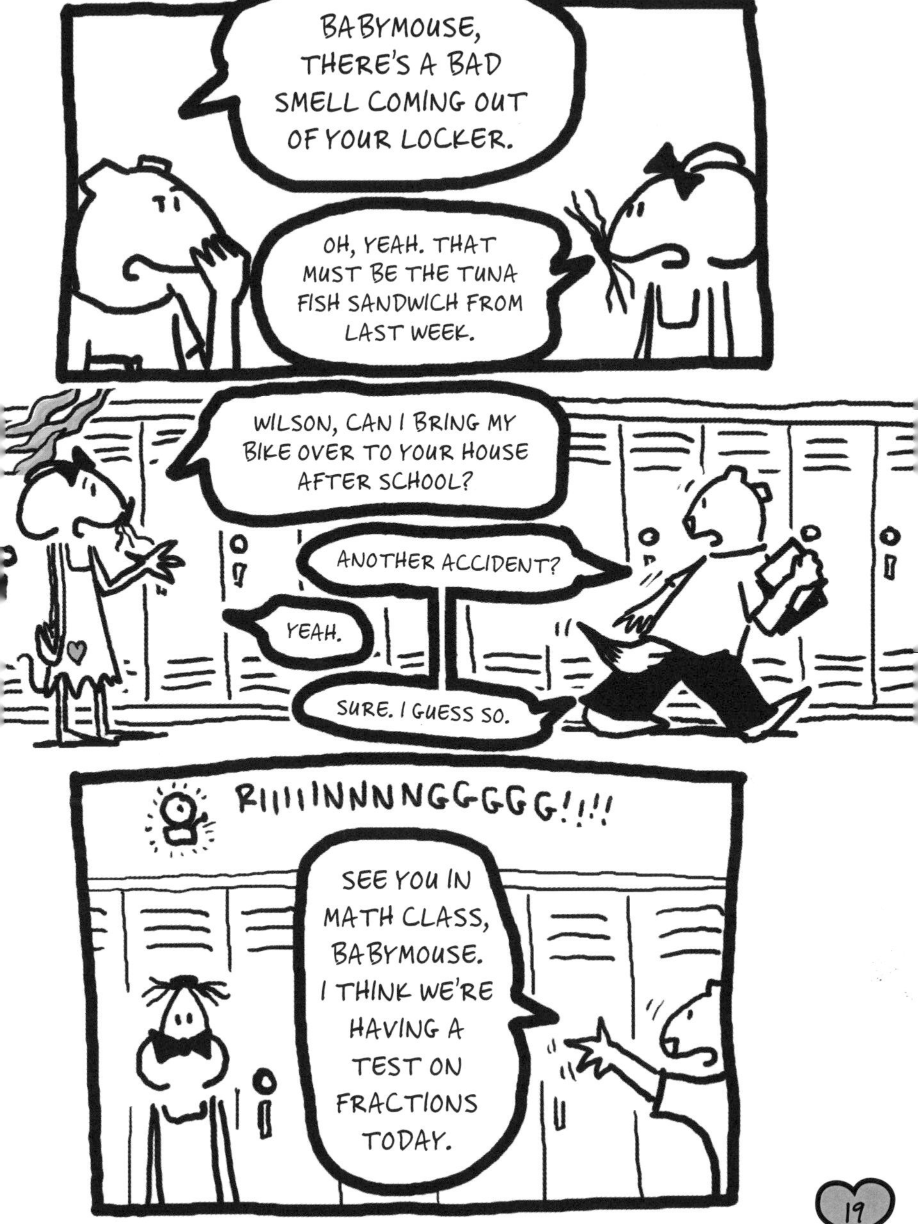
BABYMOUSE, THERE'S A BAD SMELL COMING OUT OF YOUR LOCKER.
OH, YEAH. THAT MUST BE THE TUNA FISH SANDWICH FROM LAST WEEK.
WILSON, CAN I BRING MY BIKE OVER TO YOUR HOUSE AFTER SCHOOL?
ANOTHER ACCIDENT?
YEAH.
SURE. I GUESS SO.
RIIIIINNNNGGGGG!!!!
SEE YOU IN MATH CLASS, BABYMOUSE. I THINK WE'RE HAVING A TEST ON FRACTIONS TODAY.

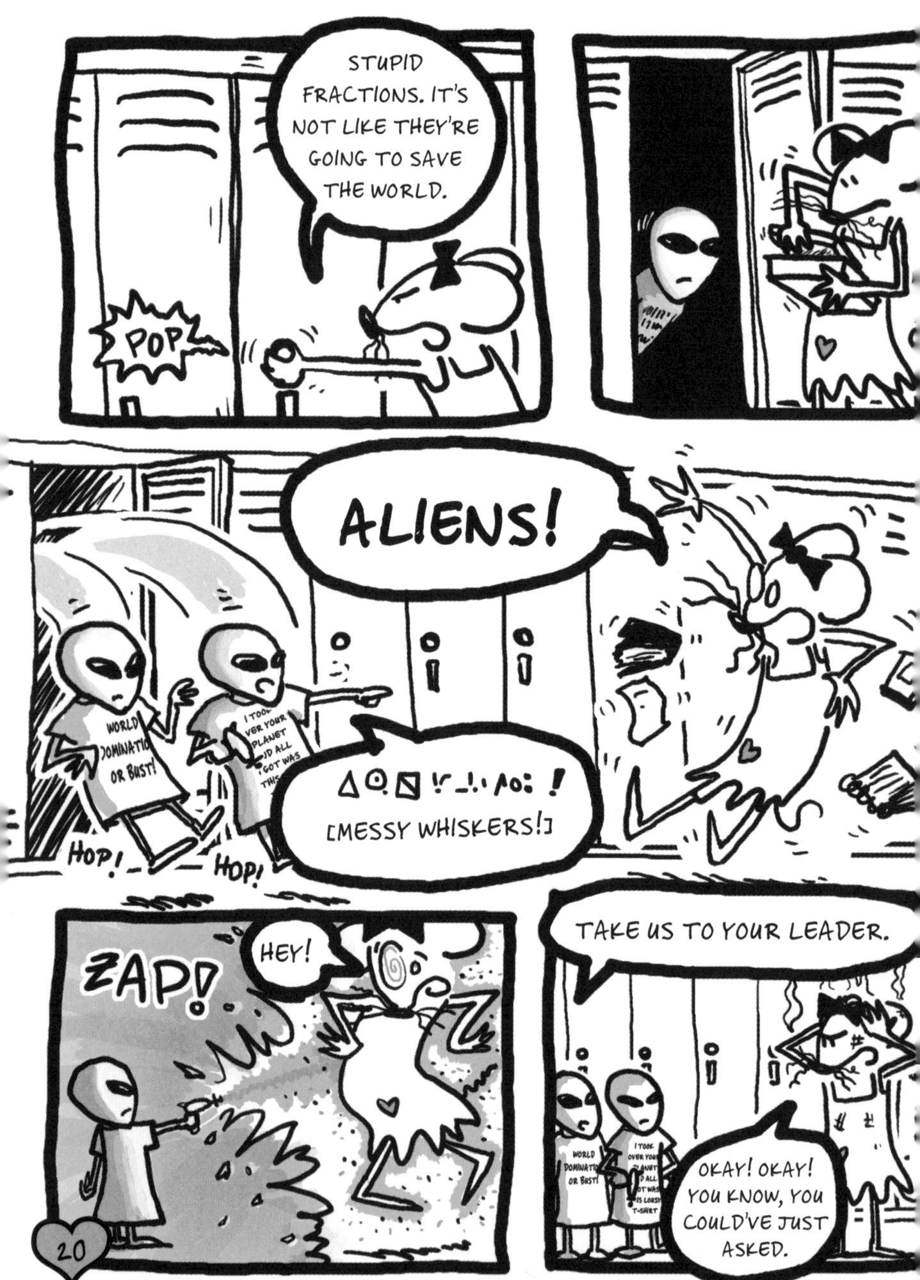
STUPID FRACTIONS. IT'S NOT LIKE THEY'RE GOING TO SAVE THE WORLD.
POP
ALIENS!
WORLD DOMINATIO OR BUST!
I TOOK OVER YOUR PLANET AND ALL I GOT WAS THIS
[MESSY WHISKERS!]
HOP!
HOP!
ZAP!
HEY!
TAKE US TO YOUR LEADER.
OKAY! OKAY! YOU KNOW, YOU COULD'VE JUST ASKED.

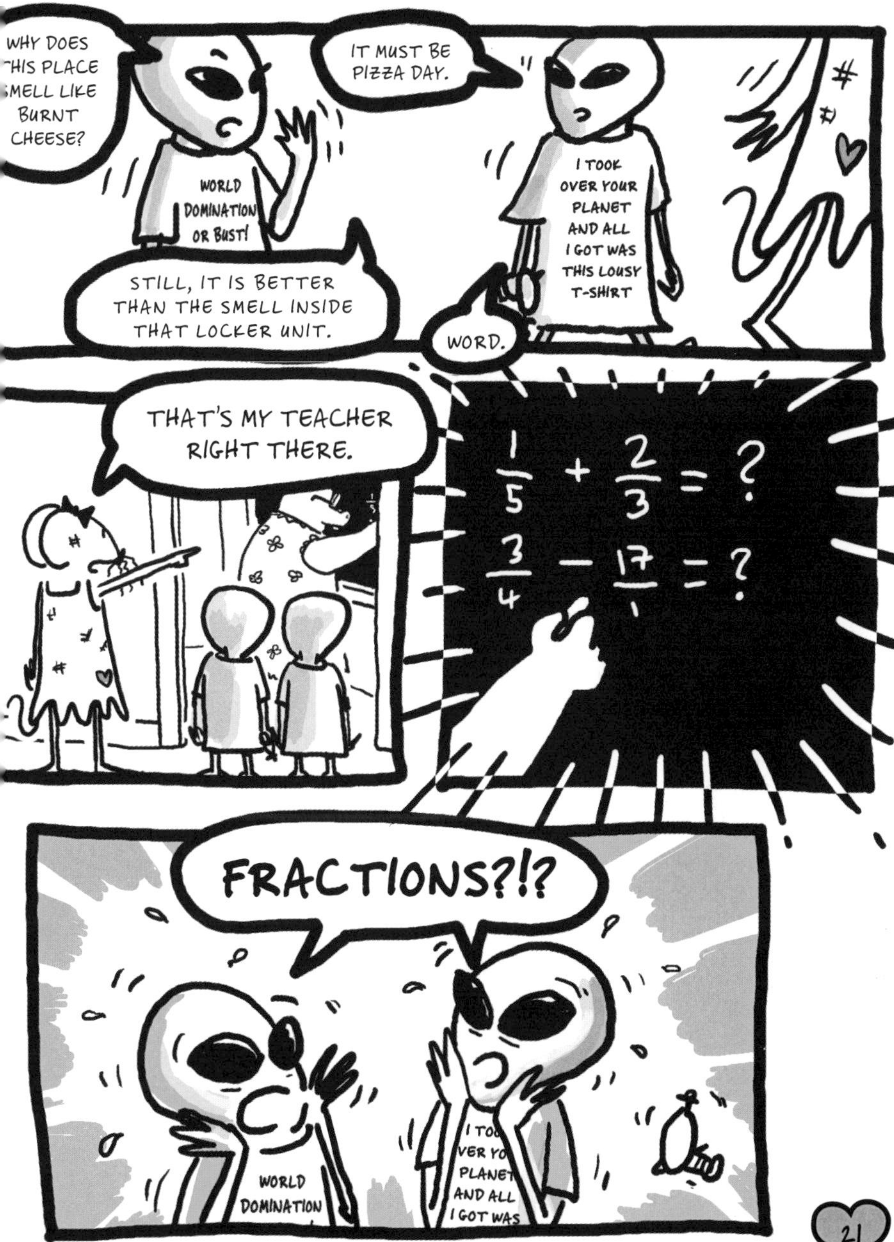
WHY DOES THIS PLACE SMELL LIKE BURNT CHEESE?
WORLD DOMINATION OR BUST!
IT MUST BE PIZZA DAY.
I TOOK OVER YOUR PLANET AND ALL I GOT WAS THIS LOUSY T-SHIRT
STILL, IT IS BETTER THAN THE SMELL INSIDE THAT LOCKER UNIT.
WORD.
THAT'S MY TEACHER RIGHT THERE.
1/5 + 2/3 = ?
3/4 − 17/1 = ?
FRACTIONS?!?
WORLD DOMINATION
I TOO VER YO PLANET AND ALL I GOT WAS

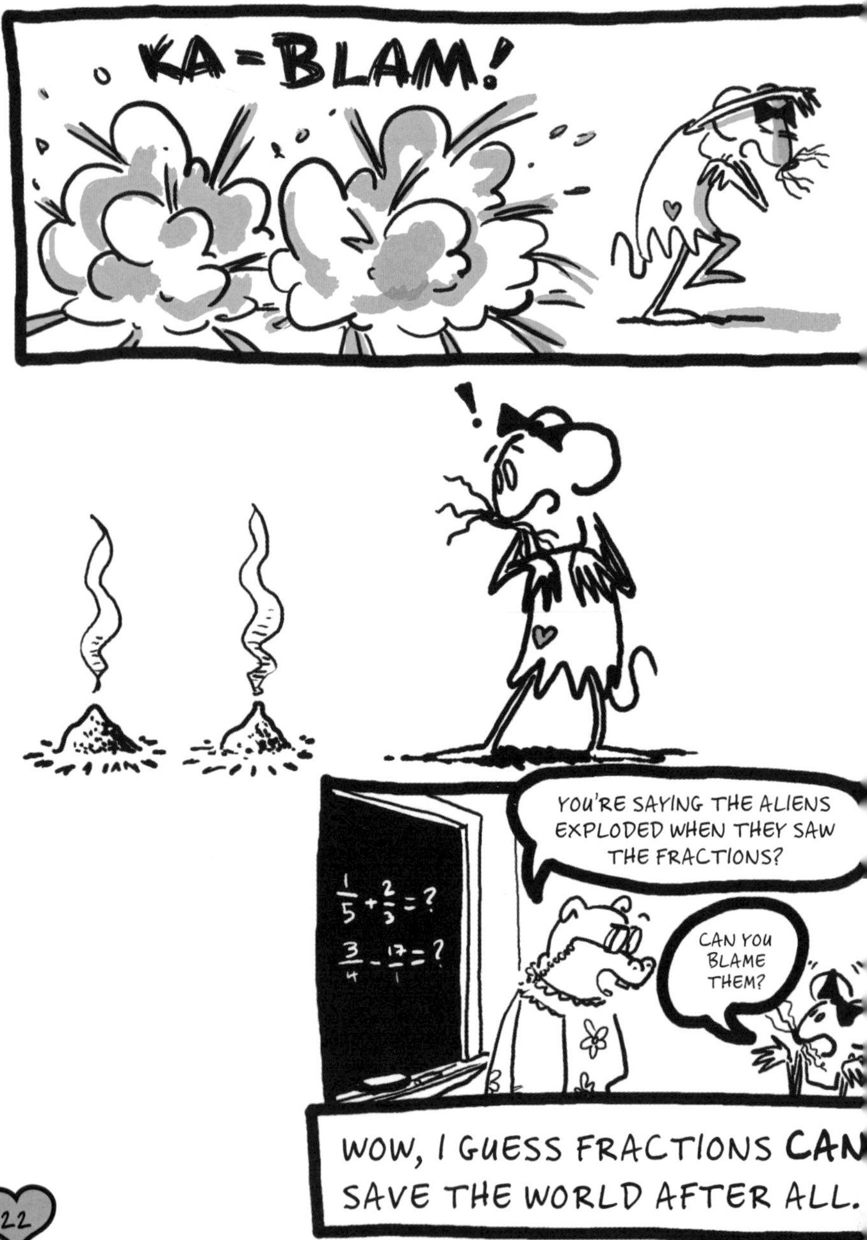
KA-BLAM!
YOU'RE SAYING THE ALIENS EXPLODED WHEN THEY SAW THE FRACTIONS?
CAN YOU BLAME THEM?
WOW, I GUESS FRACTIONS CAN SAVE THE WORLD AFTER ALL.

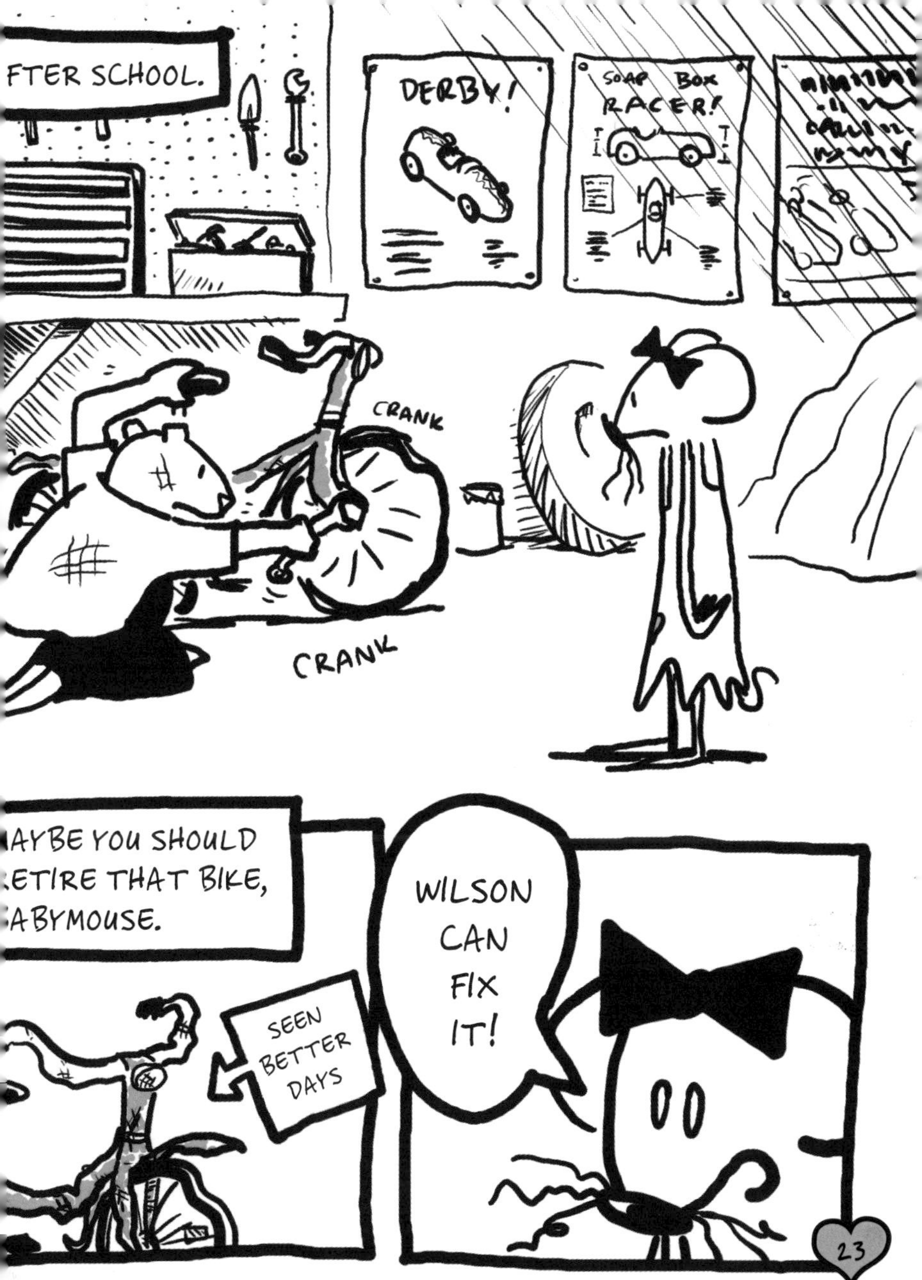

FTER SCHOOL.
DERBY!
SOAP BOX RACER!
CRANK
CRANK
AYBE YOU SHOULD ETIRE THAT BIKE, ABYMOUSE.
SEEN BETTER DAYS
WILSON CAN FIX IT!

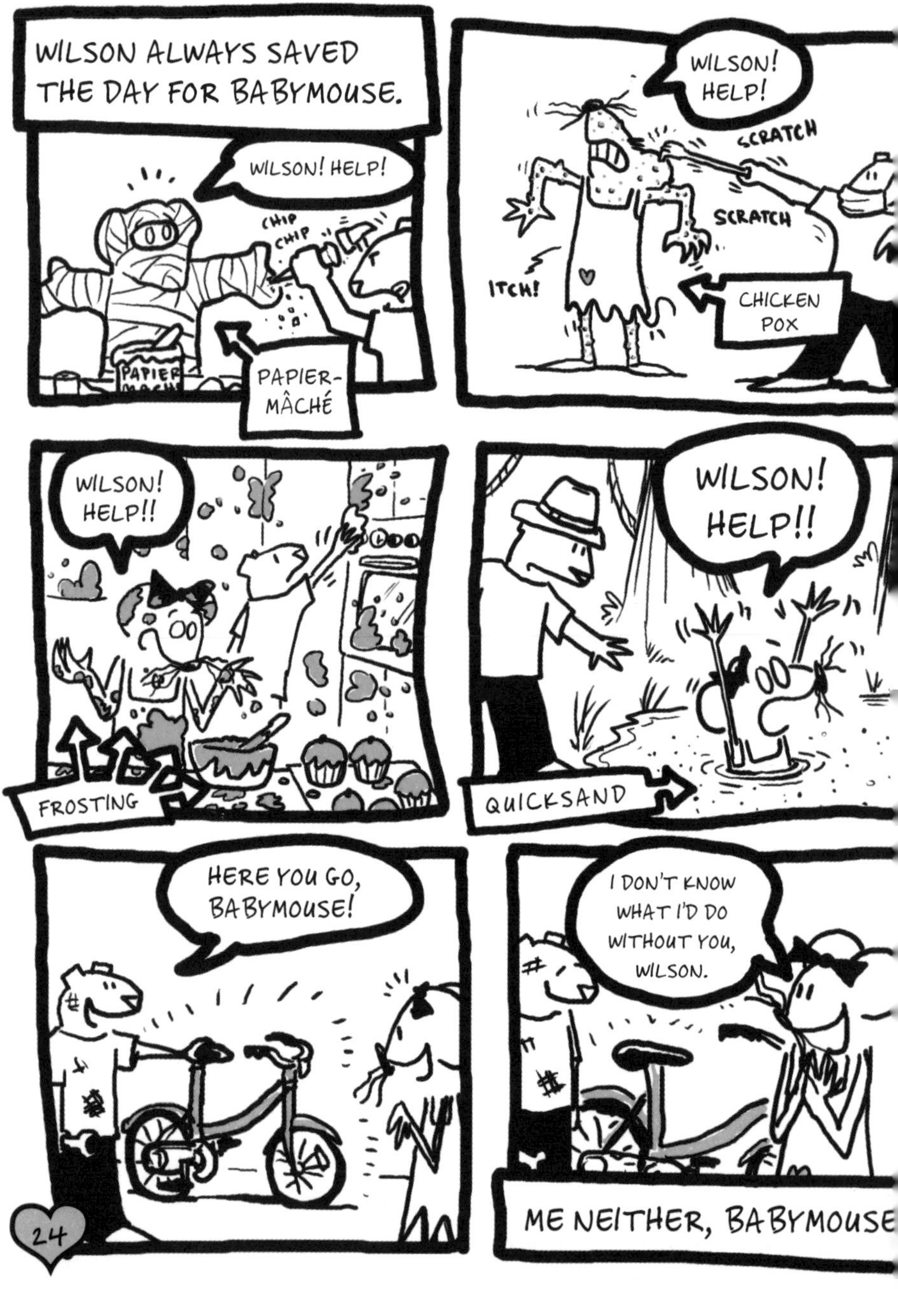
WILSON ALWAYS SAVED THE DAY FOR BABYMOUSE.
WILSON! HELP!
CHIP CHIP
PAPIER
PAPIER-MÂCHÉ
WILSON! HELP!
SCRATCH
SCRATCH
ITCH!
CHICKEN POX
WILSON! HELP!!
FROSTING
WILSON! HELP!!
QUICKSAND
HERE YOU GO, BABYMOUSE!
I DON'T KNOW WHAT I'D DO WITHOUT YOU, WILSON.
ME NEITHER, BABYMOUSE

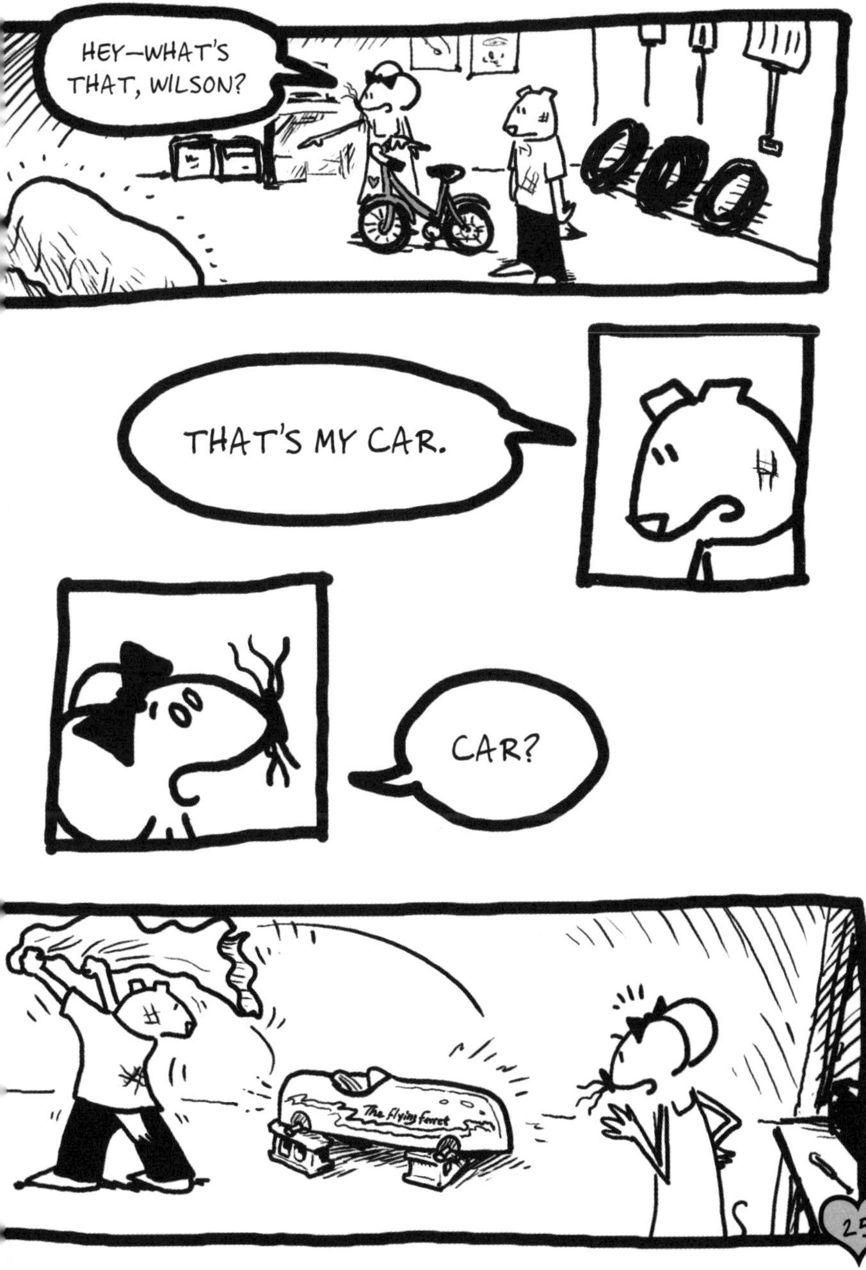
HEY—WHAT'S THAT, WILSON?
THAT'S MY CAR.
CAR?
The flying ferret

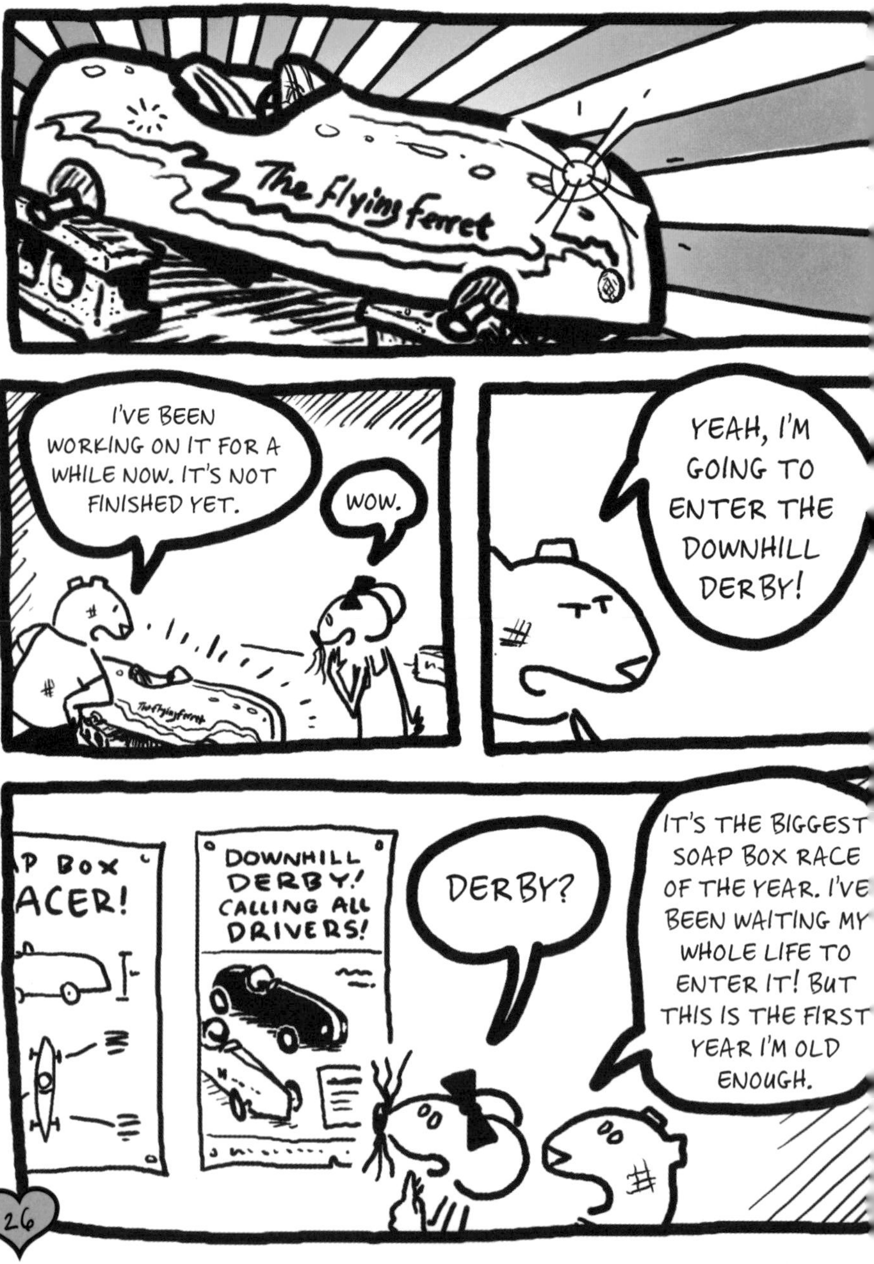
The flying ferret
I'VE BEEN WORKING ON IT FOR A WHILE NOW. IT'S NOT FINISHED YET.
WOW.
YEAH, I'M GOING TO ENTER THE DOWNHILL DERBY!
P BOX ACER!
DOWNHILL DERBY! CALLING ALL DRIVERS!
DERBY?
IT'S THE BIGGEST SOAP BOX RACE OF THE YEAR. I'VE BEEN WAITING MY WHOLE LIFE TO ENTER IT! BUT THIS IS THE FIRST YEAR I'M OLD ENOUGH.

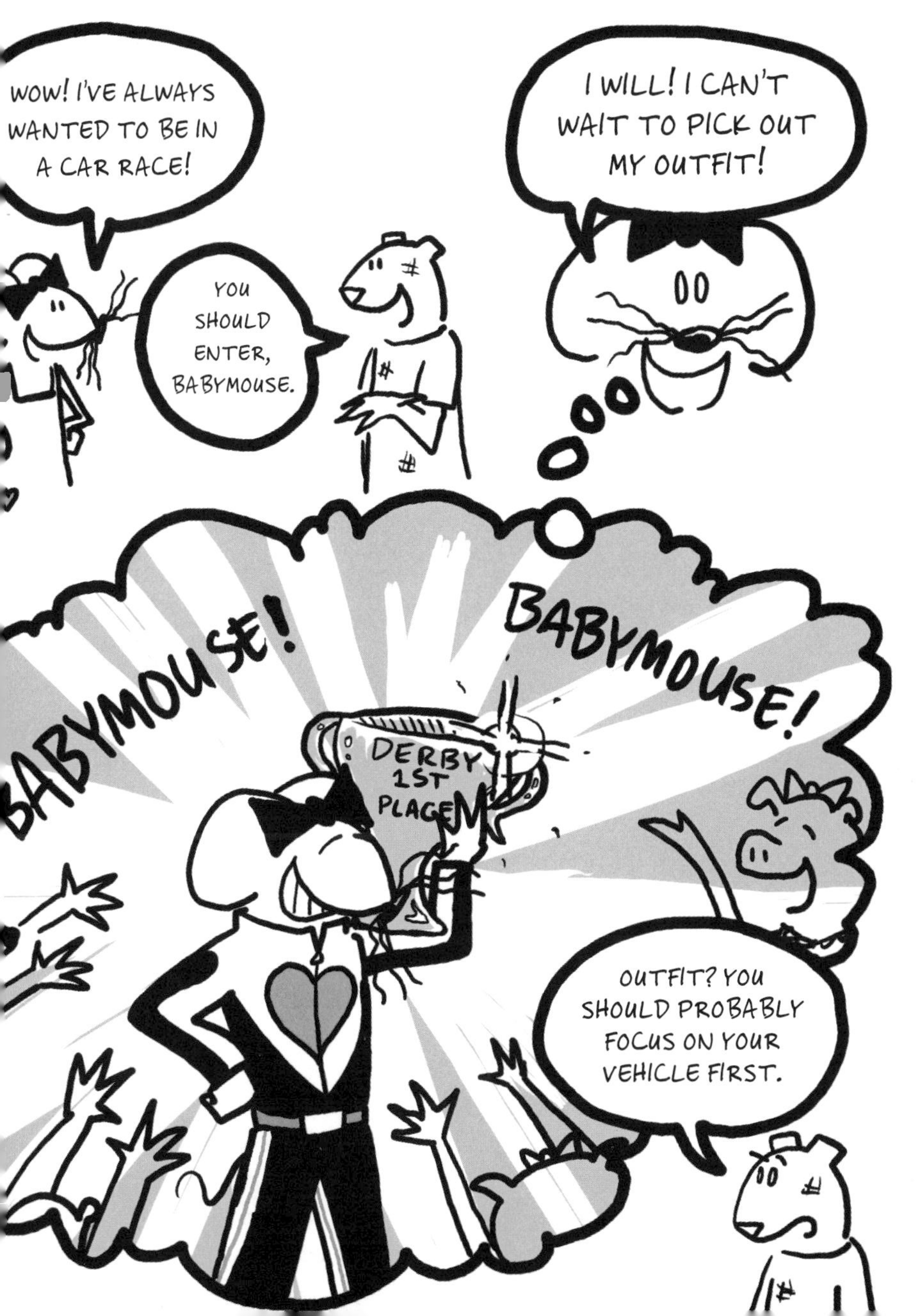
WOW! I'VE ALWAYS WANTED TO BE IN A CAR RACE!
YOU SHOULD ENTER, BABYMOUSE.
I WILL! I CAN'T WAIT TO PICK OUT MY OUTFIT!
BABYMOUSE!
BABYMOUSE!
DERBY 1ST PLACE
OUTFIT? YOU SHOULD PROBABLY FOCUS ON YOUR VEHICLE FIRST.

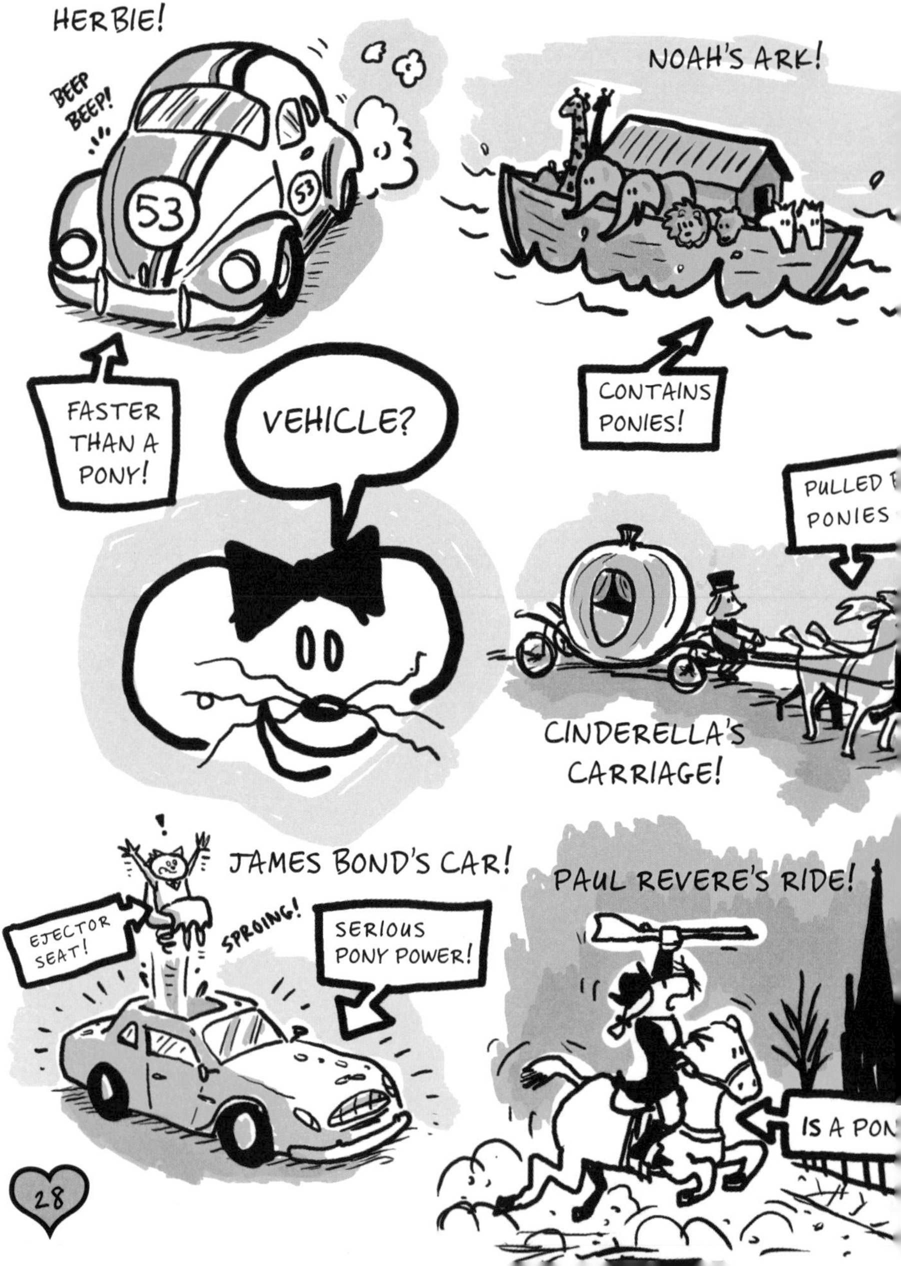

HERBIE!
BEEP BEEP!
FASTER THAN A PONY!
NOAH'S ARK!
CONTAINS PONIES!
VEHICLE?
PULLED
PONIES
CINDERELLA'S CARRIAGE!
JAMES BOND'S CAR!
EJECTOR SEAT!
SPROING!
SERIOUS PONY POWER!
PAUL REVERE'S RIDE!
IS A PON

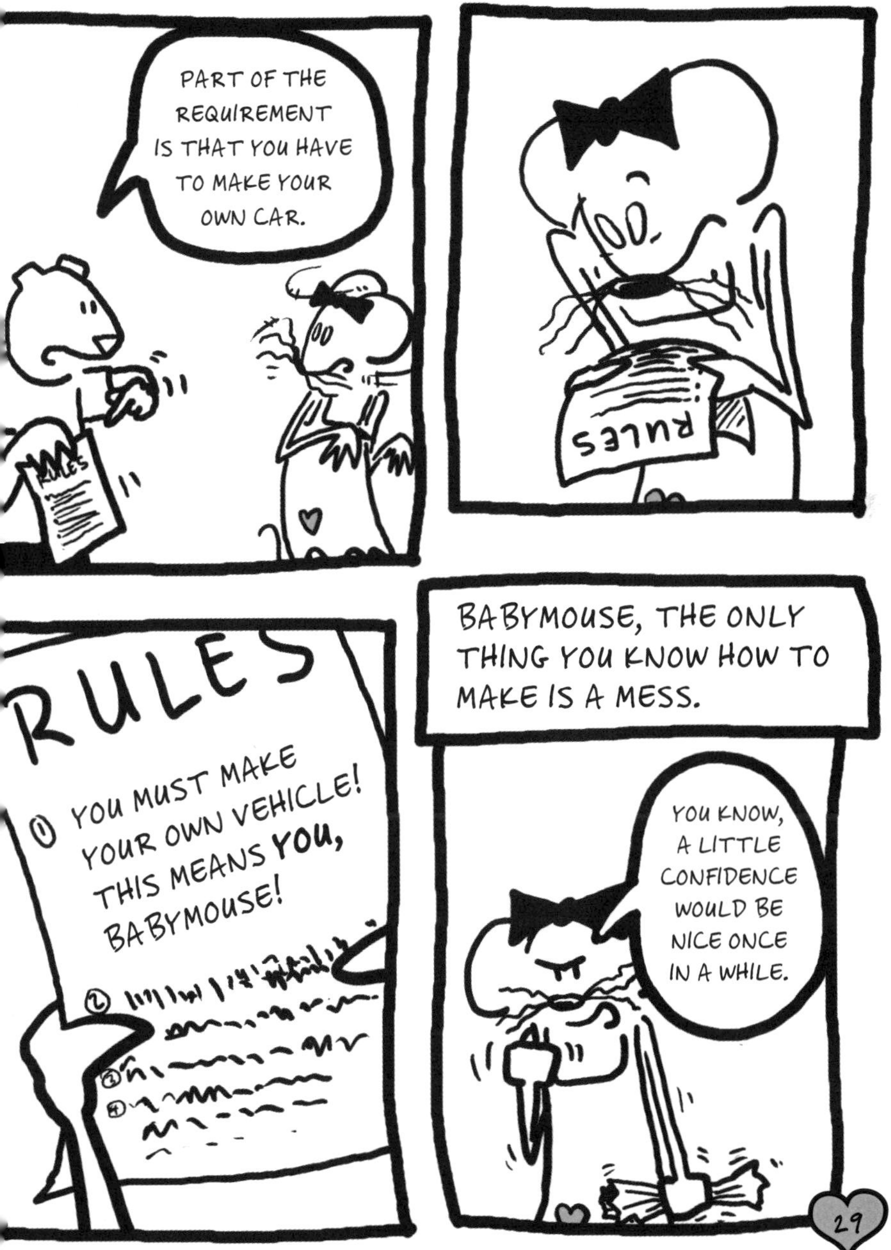
PART OF THE REQUIREMENT IS THAT YOU HAVE TO MAKE YOUR OWN CAR.
RULES
RULES
RULES
① YOU MUST MAKE YOUR OWN VEHICLE! THIS MEANS **YOU**, BABYMOUSE!
BABYMOUSE, THE ONLY THING YOU KNOW HOW TO MAKE IS A MESS.
YOU KNOW, A LITTLE CONFIDENCE WOULD BE NICE ONCE IN A WHILE.

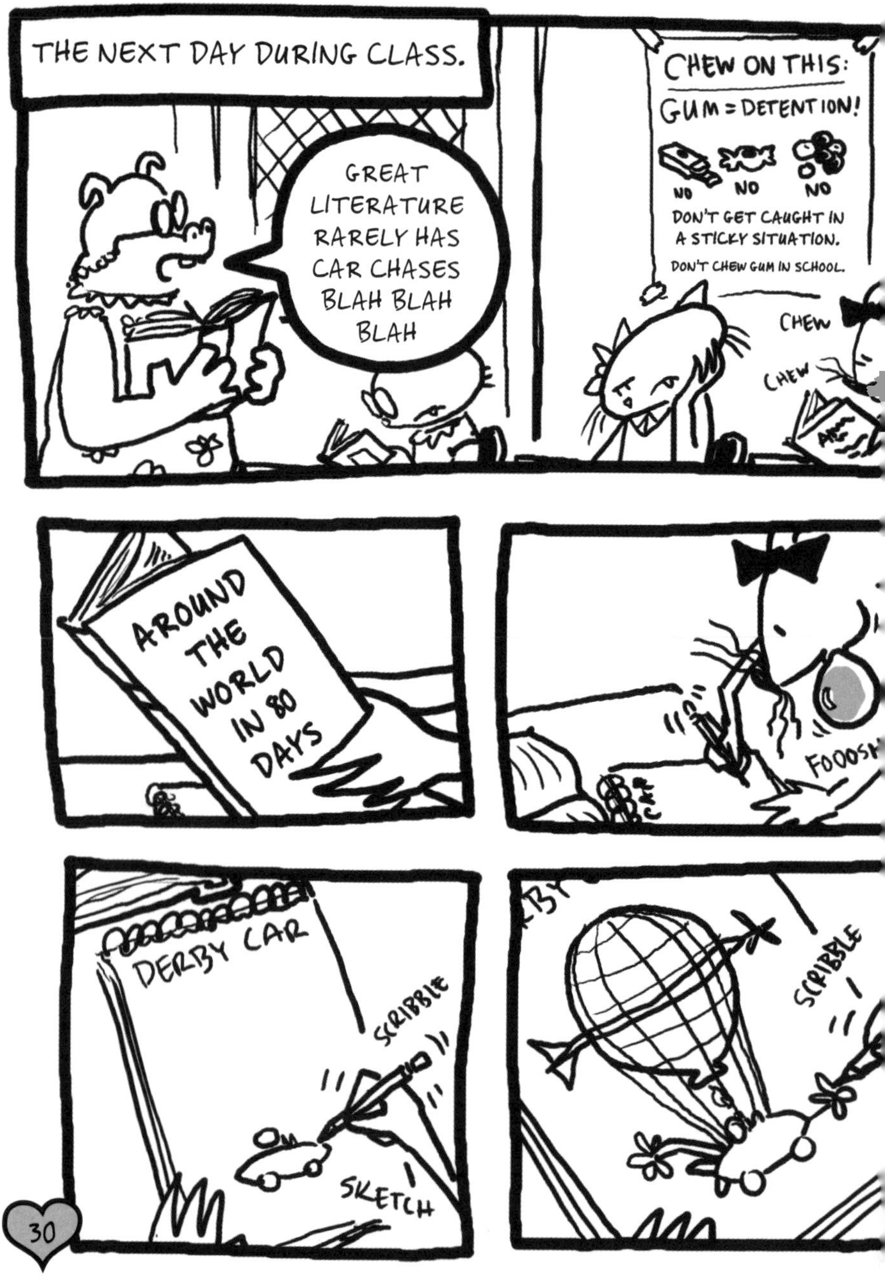
THE NEXT DAY DURING CLASS.
GREAT LITERATURE RARELY HAS CAR CHASES BLAH BLAH BLAH
CHEW ON THIS:
GUM = DETENTION!
NO NO NO
DON'T GET CAUGHT IN A STICKY SITUATION.
DON'T CHEW GUM IN SCHOOL.
CHEW
CHEW
AROUND THE WORLD IN 80 DAYS
DERBY CAR
SCRIBBLE
SKETCH
SCRIBBLE

Around the School

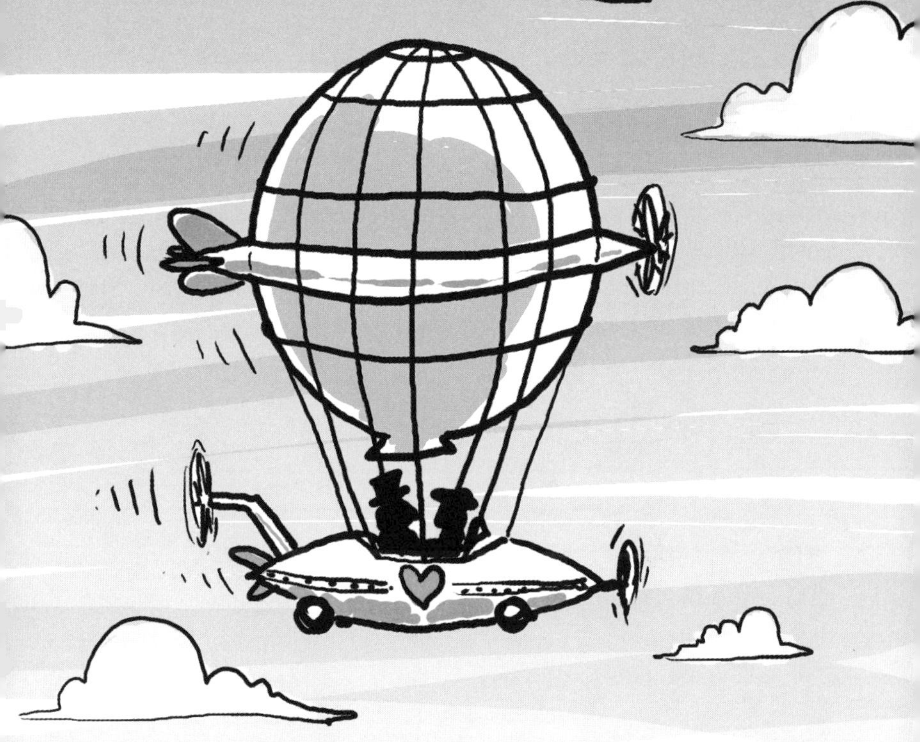

in 8 Periods!

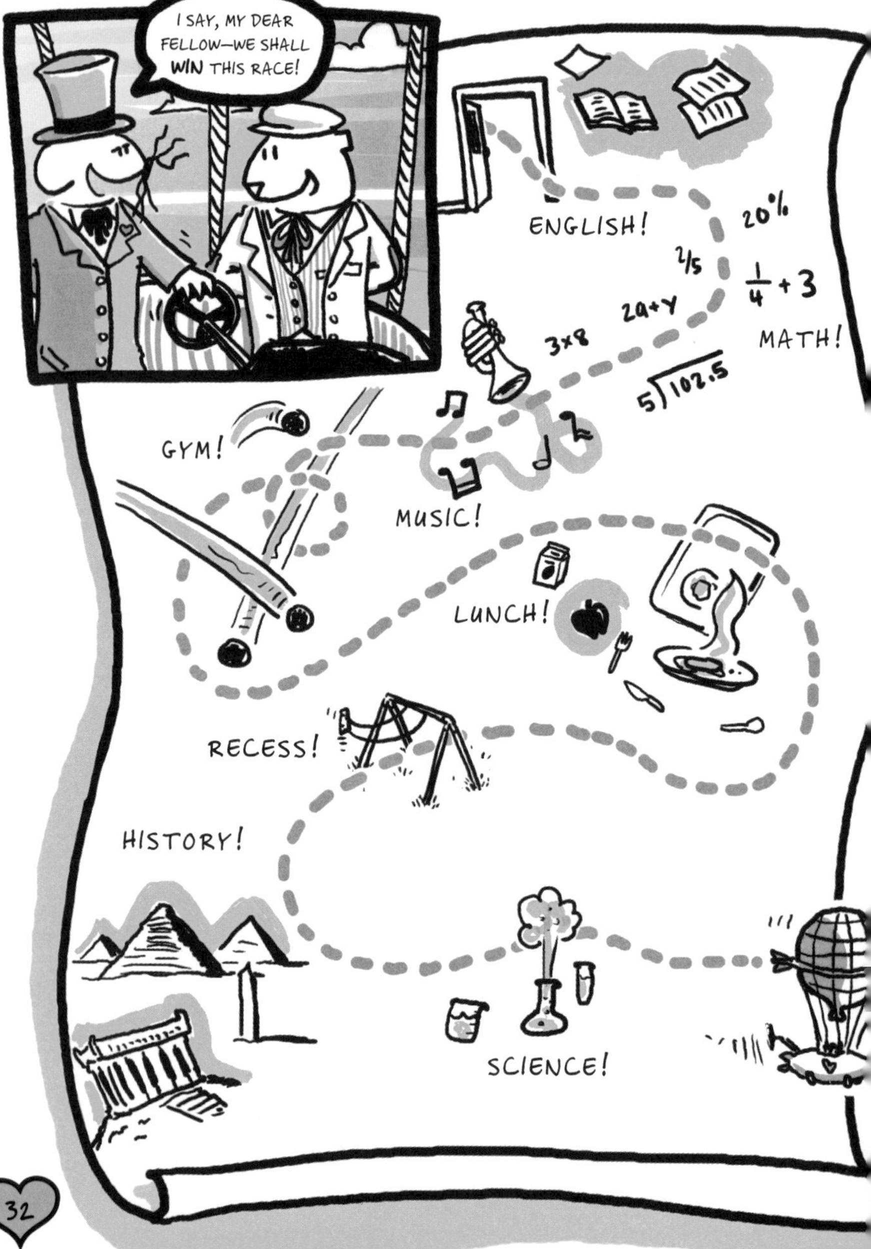
I SAY, MY DEAR FELLOW—WE SHALL **WIN** THIS RACE!
ENGLISH!
20%
2/5
1/4 + 3
2a+Y
3x8
MATH!
5)102.5
GYM!
MUSIC!
LUNCH!
RECESS!
HISTORY!
SCIENCE!

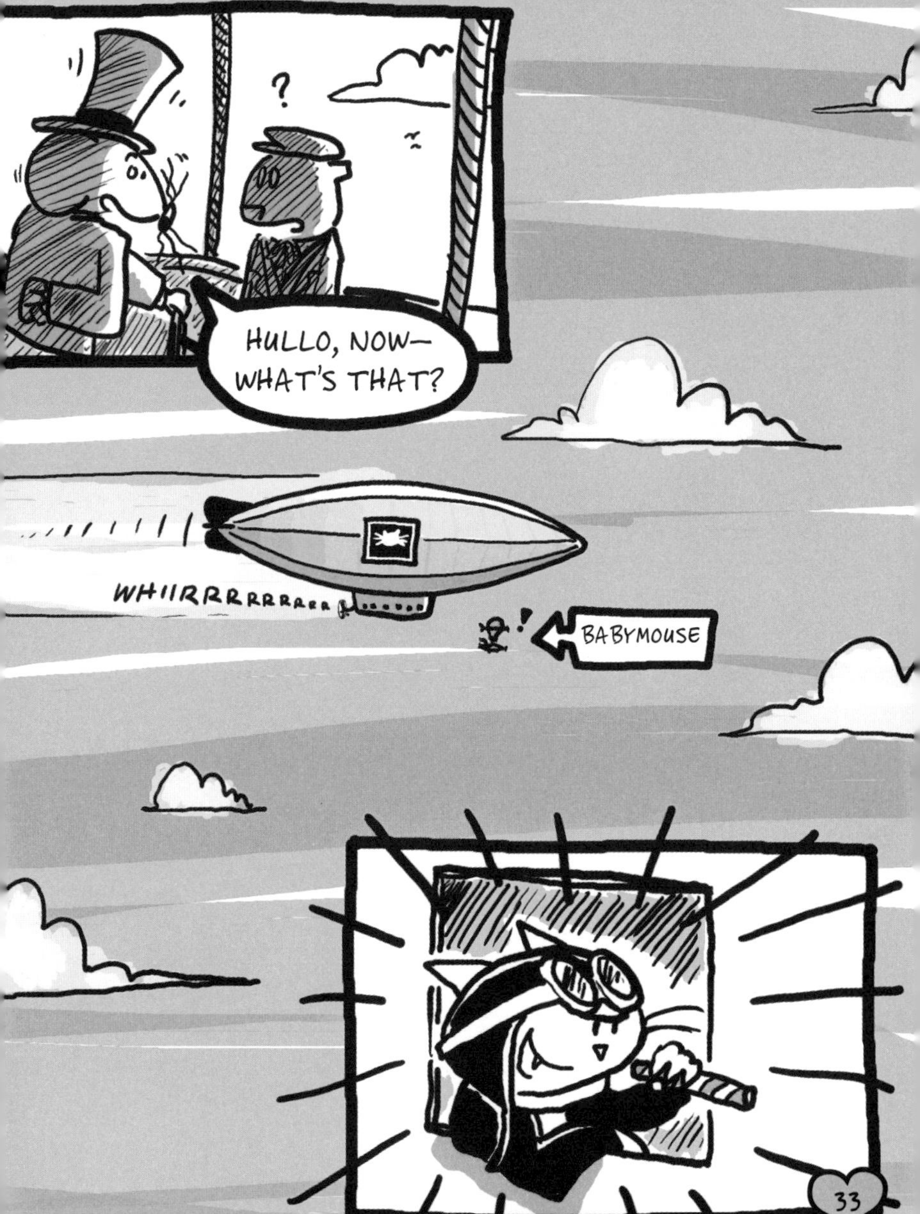
HULLO, NOW—
WHAT'S THAT?
WHIIRRRRRRRRRR
BABYMOUSE

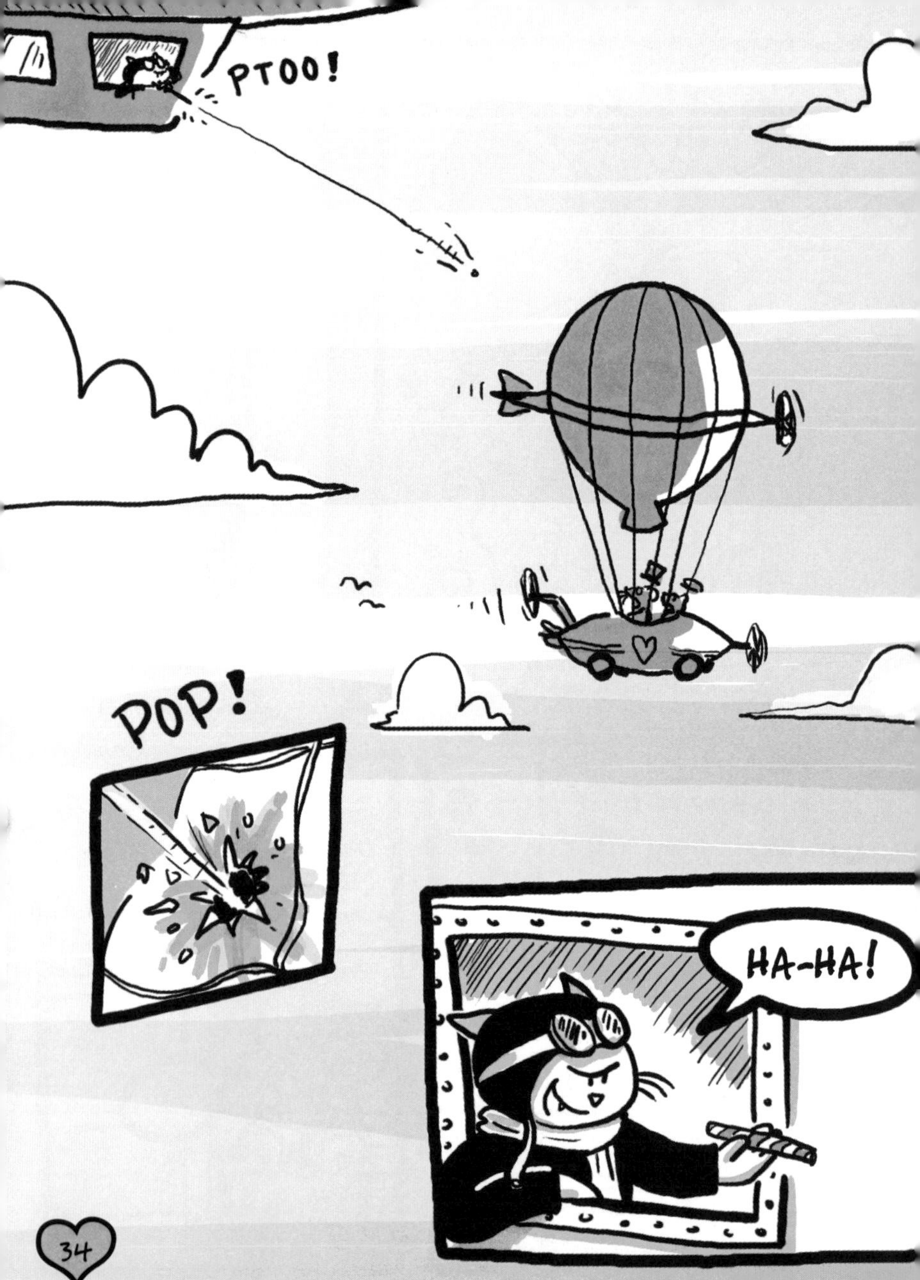
PTOO!
POP!
HA-HA!

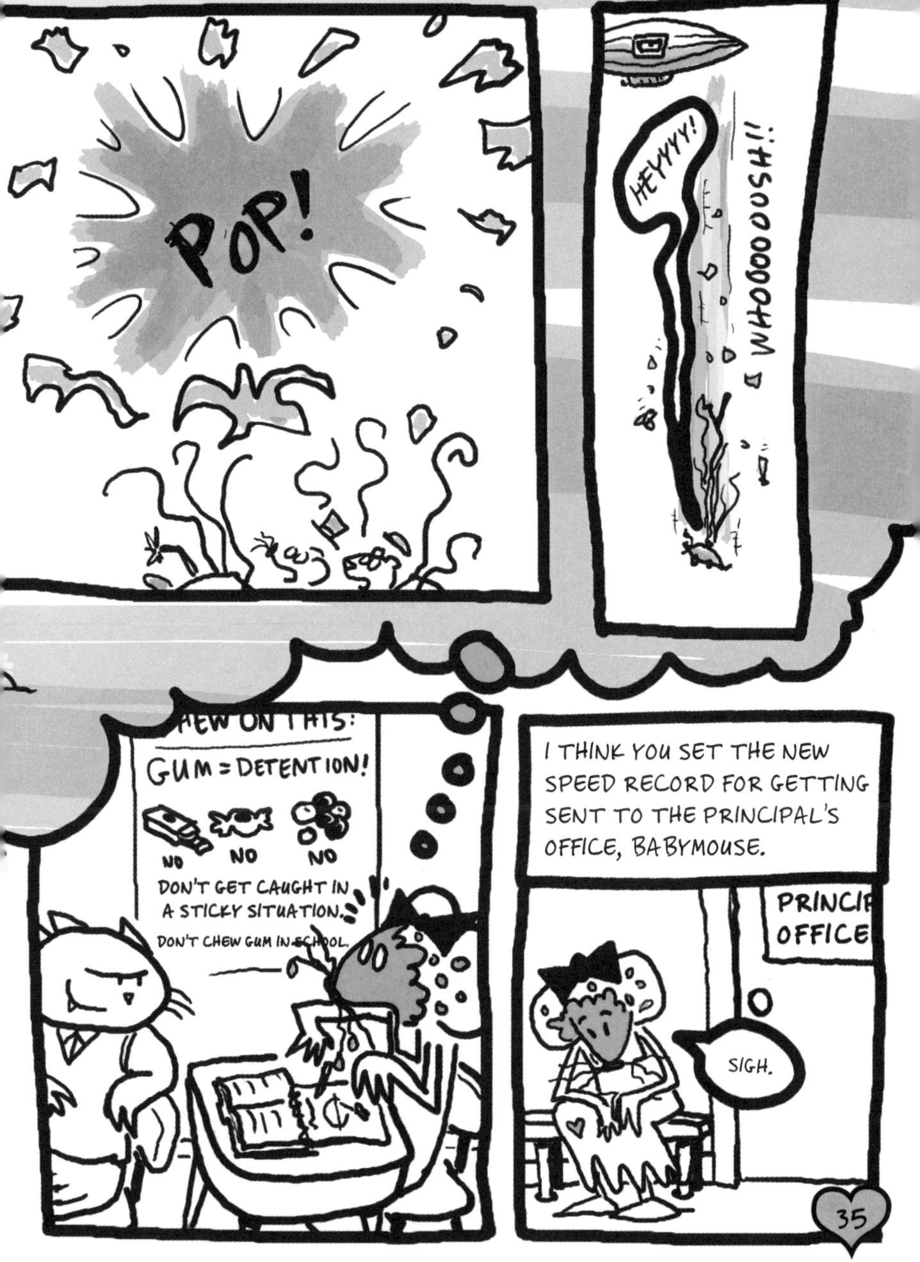
POP!
HEYYYY!
WHOOOOOOSH!!
HEW ON THIS:
GUM = DETENTION!
NO NO NO
DON'T GET CAUGHT IN A STICKY SITUATION.
DON'T CHEW GUM IN SCHOOL.
I THINK YOU SET THE NEW SPEED RECORD FOR GETTING SENT TO THE PRINCIPAL'S OFFICE, BABYMOUSE.
PRINCI
OFFICE
SIGH.

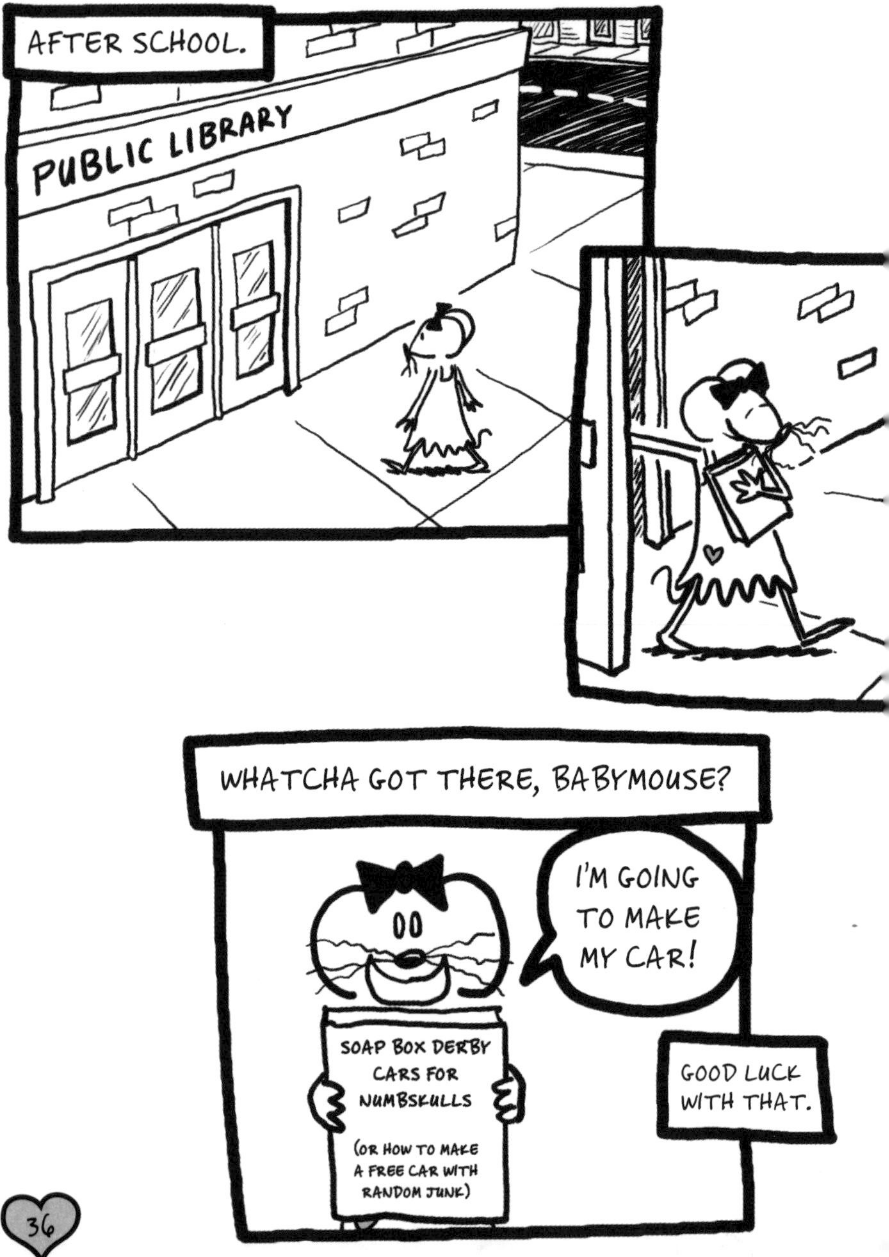
AFTER SCHOOL.
PUBLIC LIBRARY
WHATCHA GOT THERE, BABYMOUSE?
I'M GOING TO MAKE MY CAR!
SOAP BOX DERBY CARS FOR NUMBSKULLS
(OR HOW TO MAKE A FREE CAR WITH RANDOM JUNK)
GOOD LUCK WITH THAT.

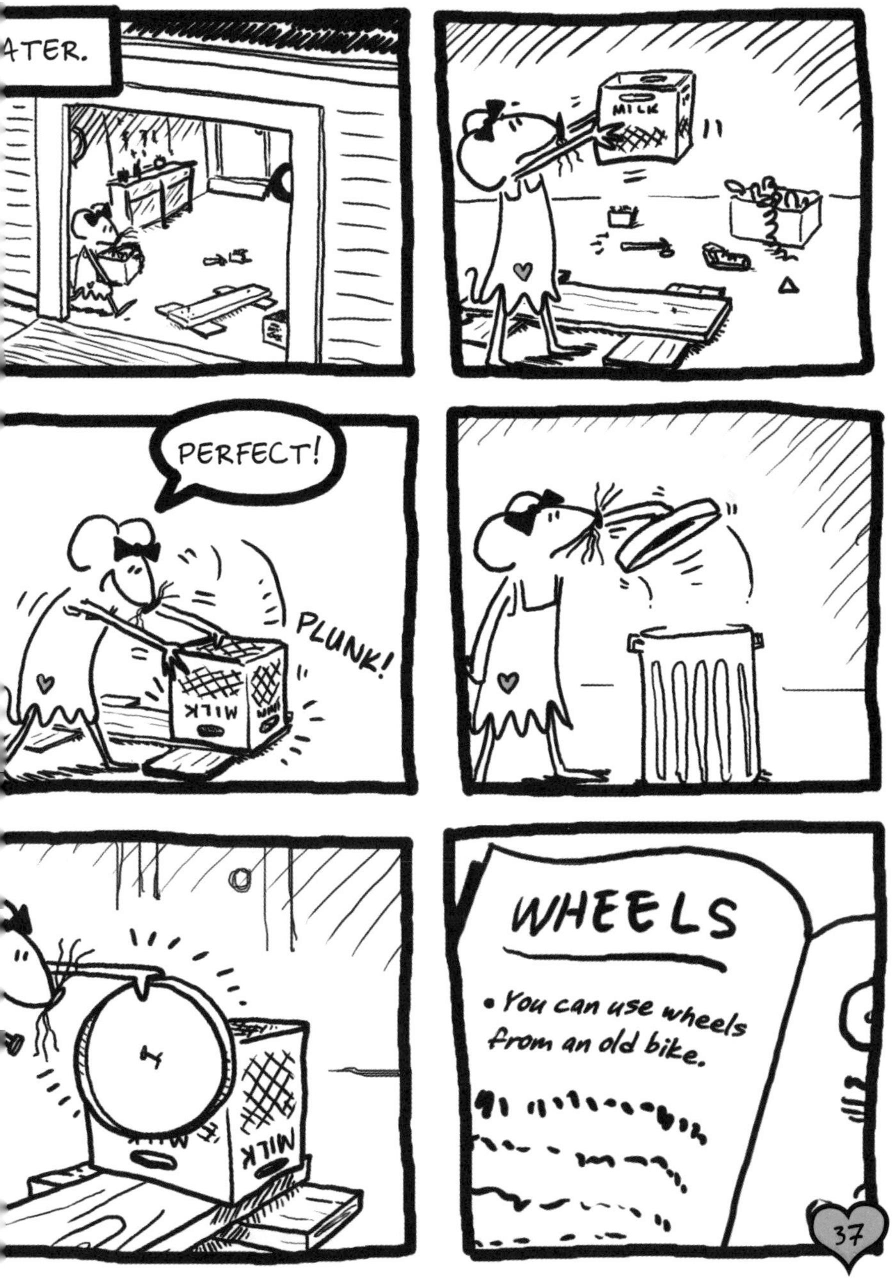
ATER.
MILK
PERFECT!
PLUNK!
MILK
MILK
WHEELS
• You can use wheels from an old bike.
37

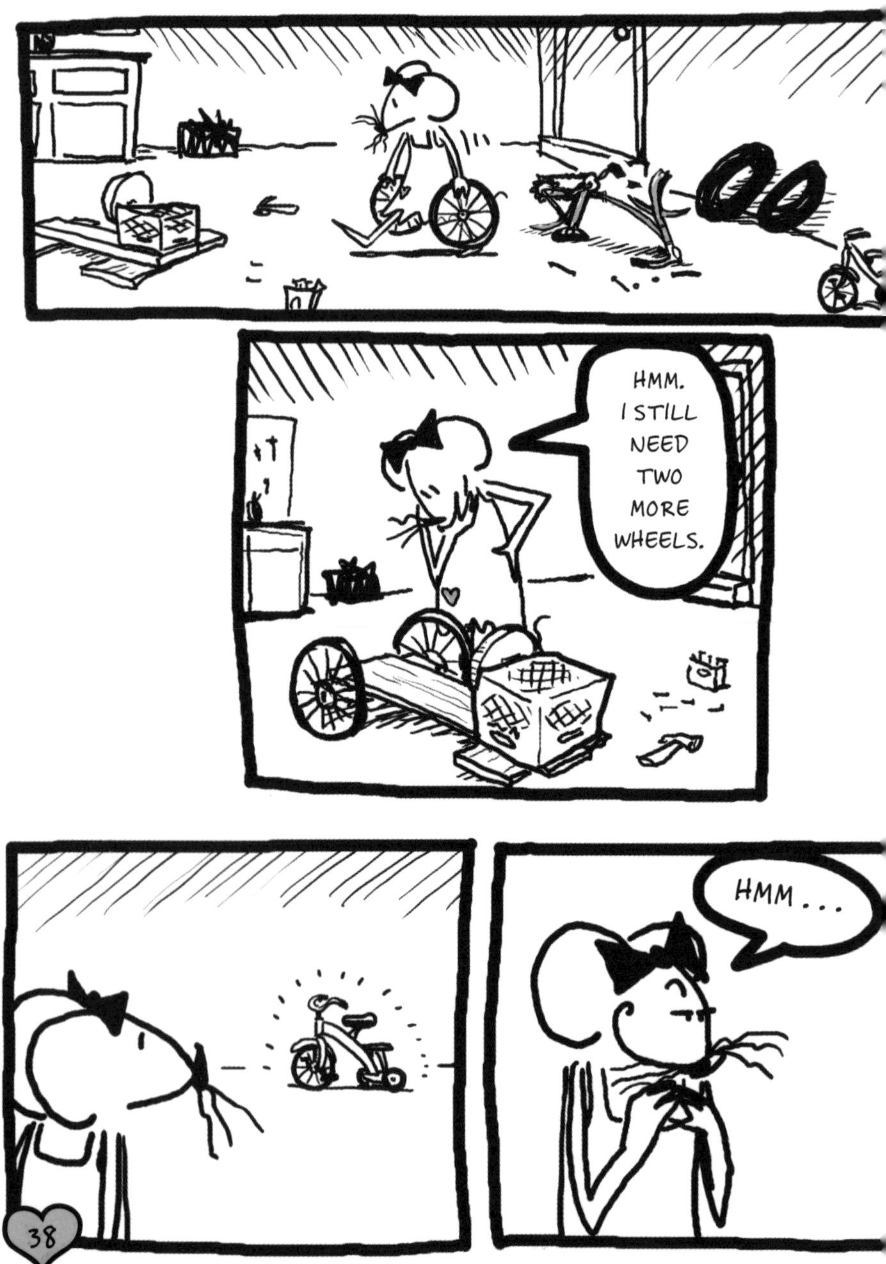
HMM. I STILL NEED TWO MORE WHEELS.
HMM...

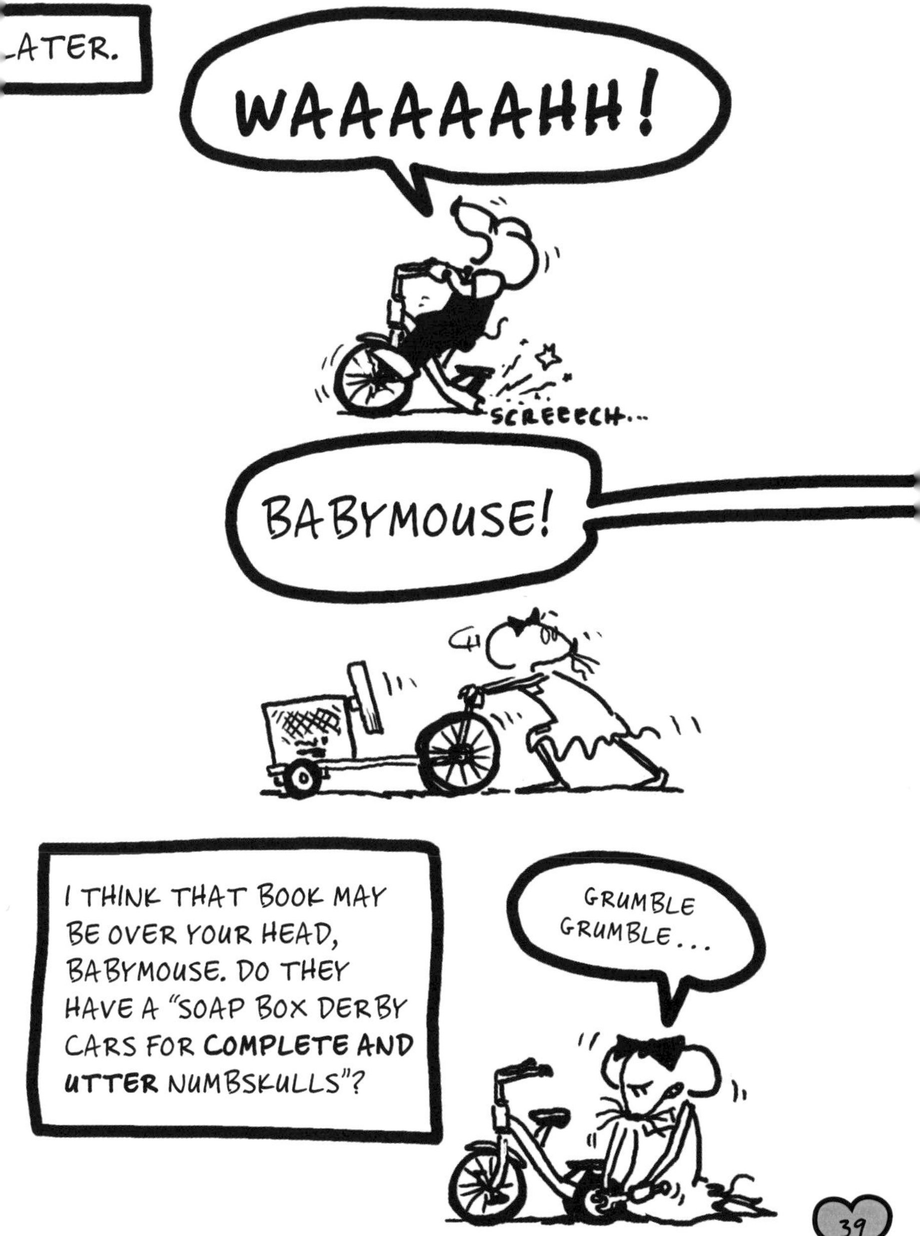

LATER.
WAAAAAHH!
SCREEECH...
BABYMOUSE!
I THINK THAT BOOK MAY BE OVER YOUR HEAD, BABYMOUSE. DO THEY HAVE A "SOAP BOX DERBY CARS FOR **COMPLETE AND UTTER** NUMBSKULLS"?
GRUMBLE GRUMBLE...

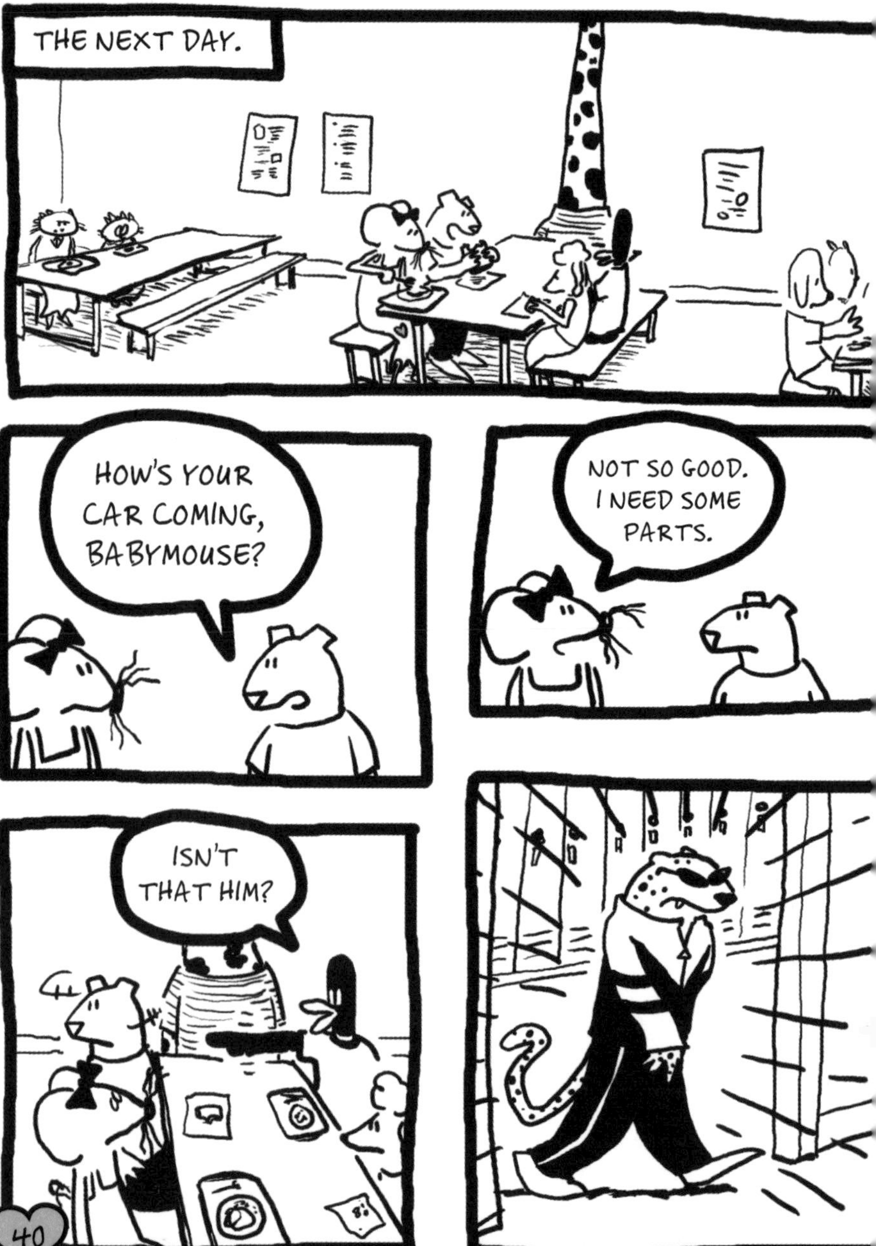
THE NEXT DAY.
HOW'S YOUR CAR COMING, BABYMOUSE?
NOT SO GOOD. I NEED SOME PARTS.
ISN'T THAT HIM?

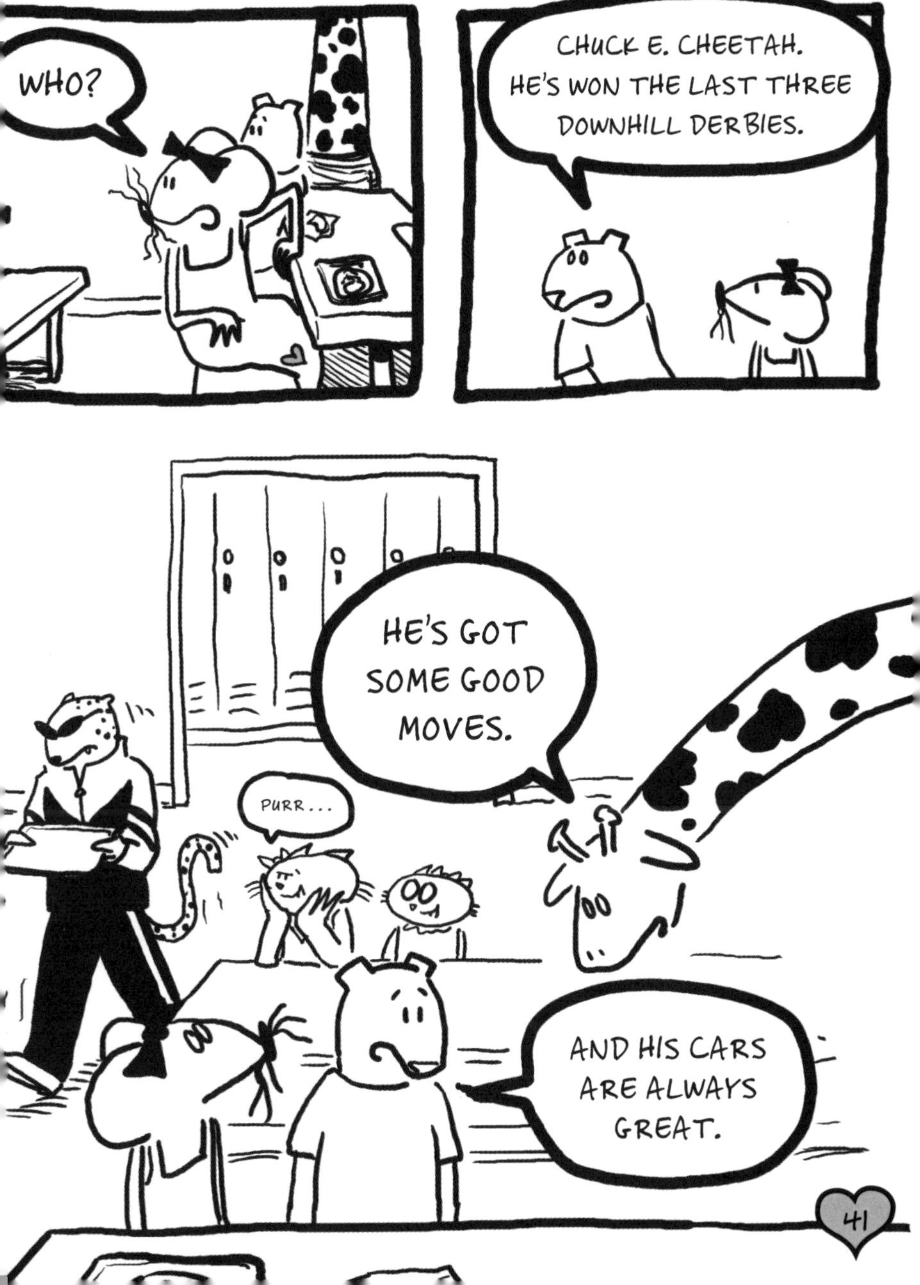
WHO?
CHUCK E. CHEETAH. HE'S WON THE LAST THREE DOWNHILL DERBIES.
HE'S GOT SOME GOOD MOVES.
PURR...
AND HIS CARS ARE ALWAYS GREAT.

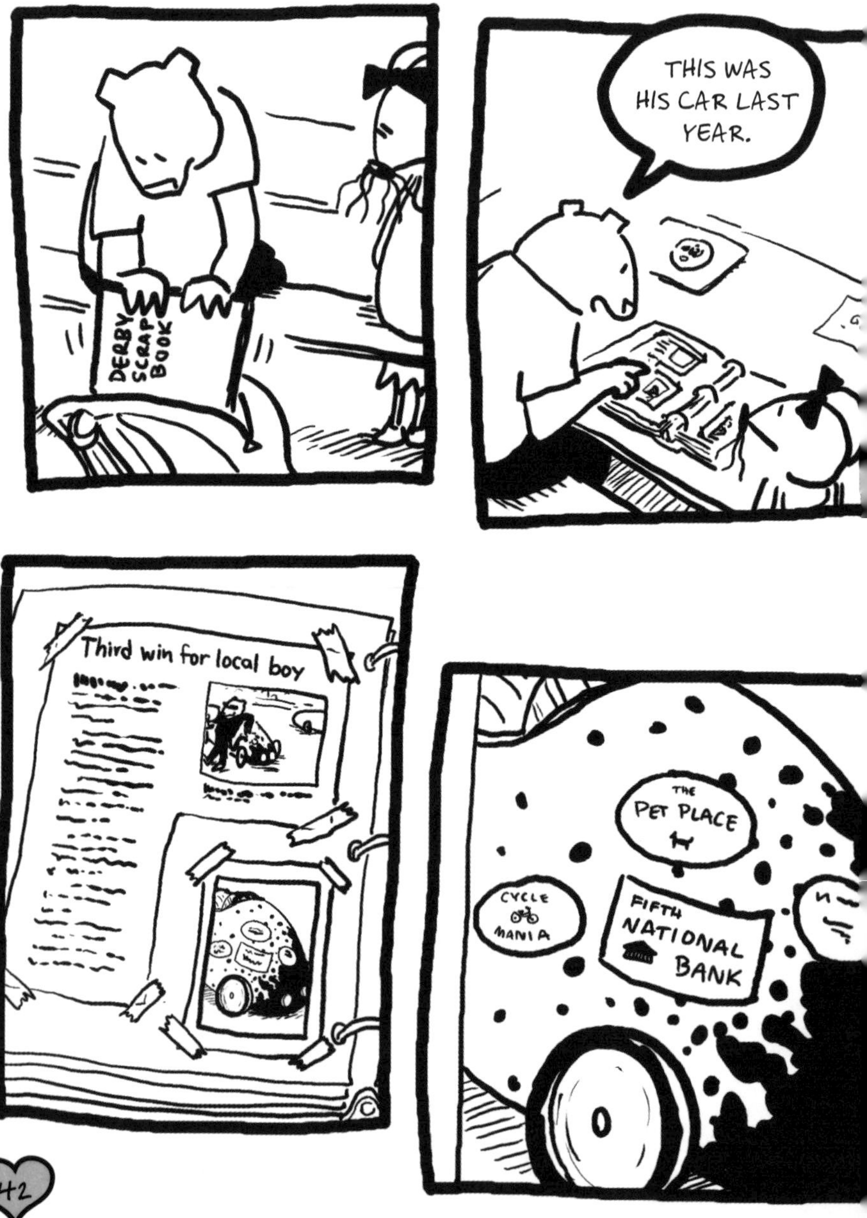
DERBY SCRAP BOOK
THIS WAS HIS CAR LAST YEAR.
Third win for local boy
THE PET PLACE
CYCLE MANIA
FIFTH NATIONAL BANK

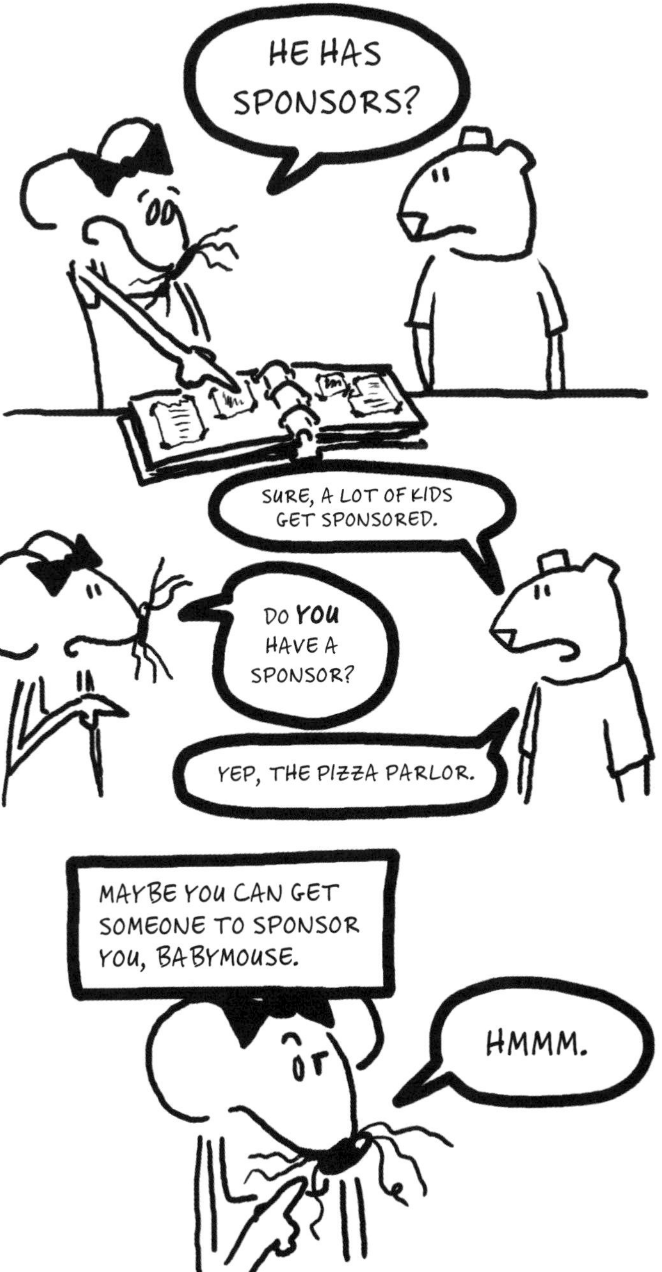
HE HAS SPONSORS?
SURE, A LOT OF KIDS GET SPONSORED.
DO **YOU** HAVE A SPONSOR?
YEP, THE PIZZA PARLOR.
MAYBE YOU CAN GET SOMEONE TO SPONSOR YOU, BABYMOUSE.
HMMM.

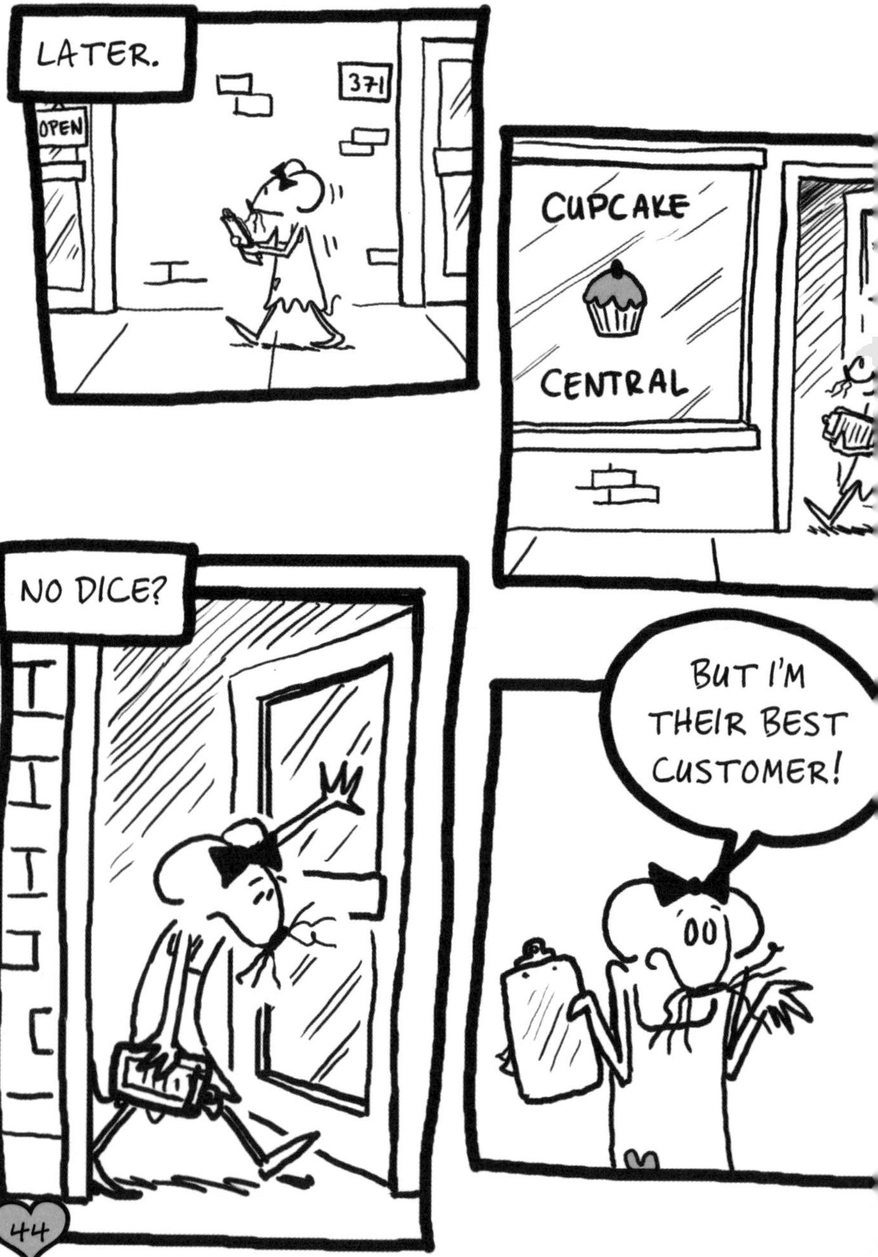
LATER.
371
OPEN
CUPCAKE
CENTRAL
NO DICE?
BUT I'M THEIR BEST CUSTOMER!

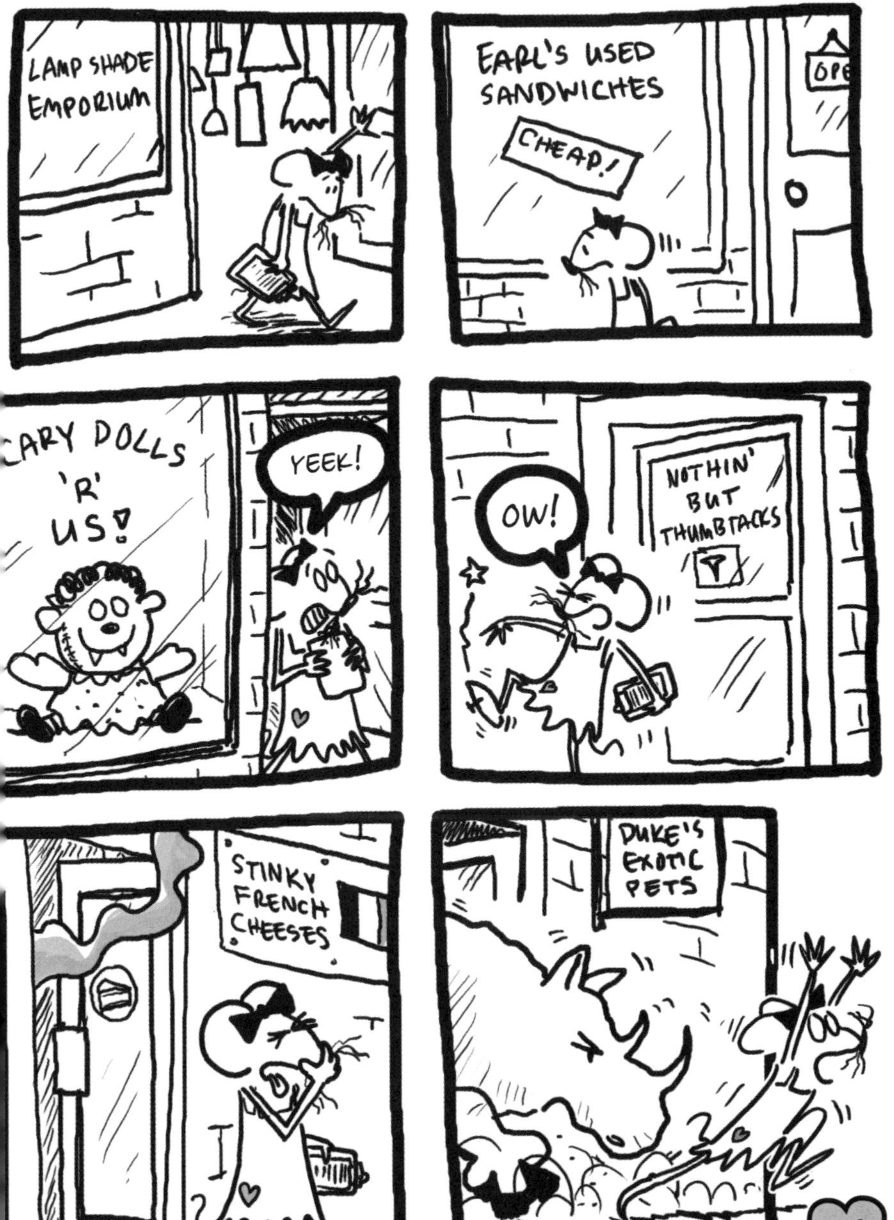
LAMP SHADE EMPORIUM
EARL'S USED SANDWICHES
CHEAP!
OPE
CARY DOLLS 'R' US!
YEEK!
OW!
NOTHIN' BUT THUMBTACKS
STINKY FRENCH CHEESES
DUKE'S EXOTIC PETS

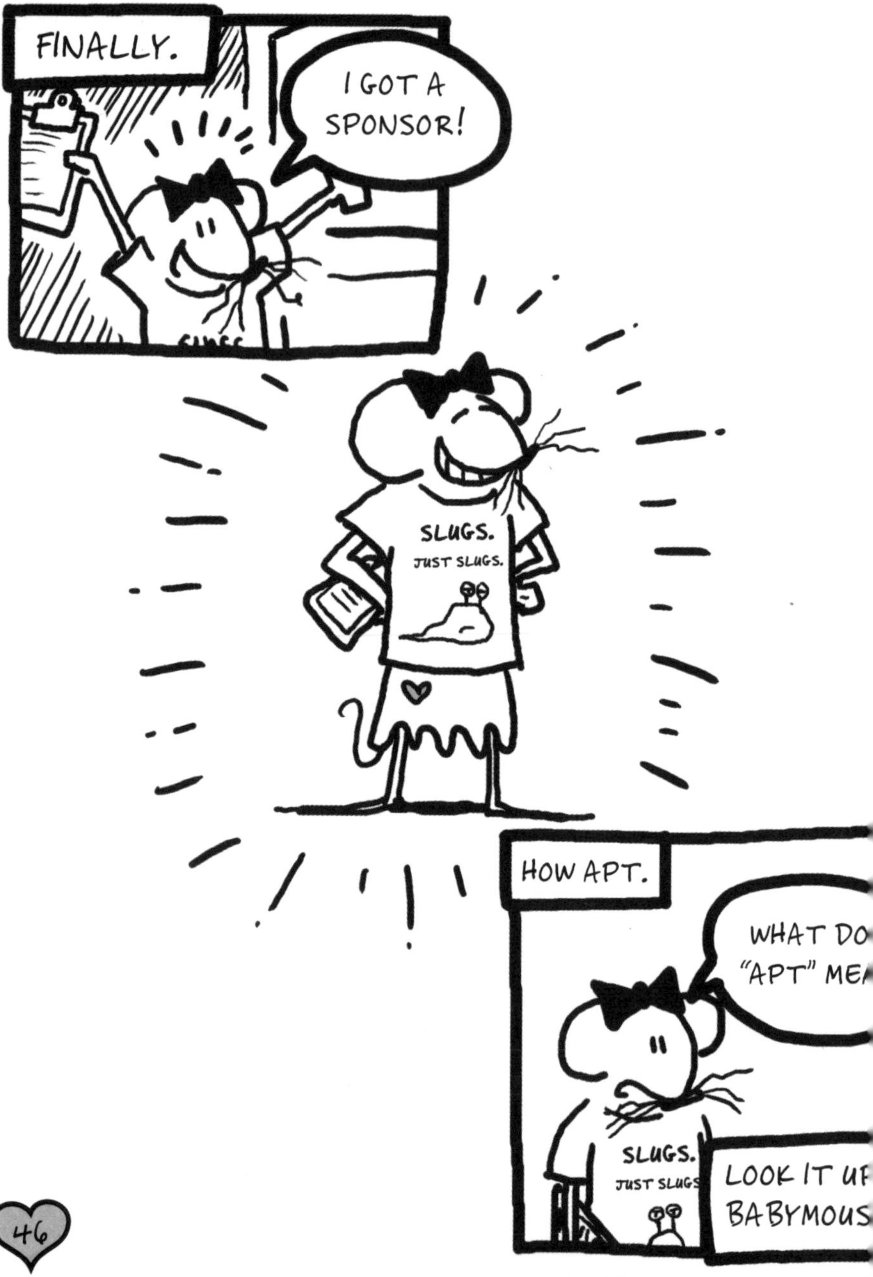
FINALLY.
I GOT A SPONSOR!
SLUGS.
SLUGS. JUST SLUGS.
HOW APT.
WHAT DO "APT" ME
SLUGS. JUST SLUGS
LOOK IT U BABYMOUS

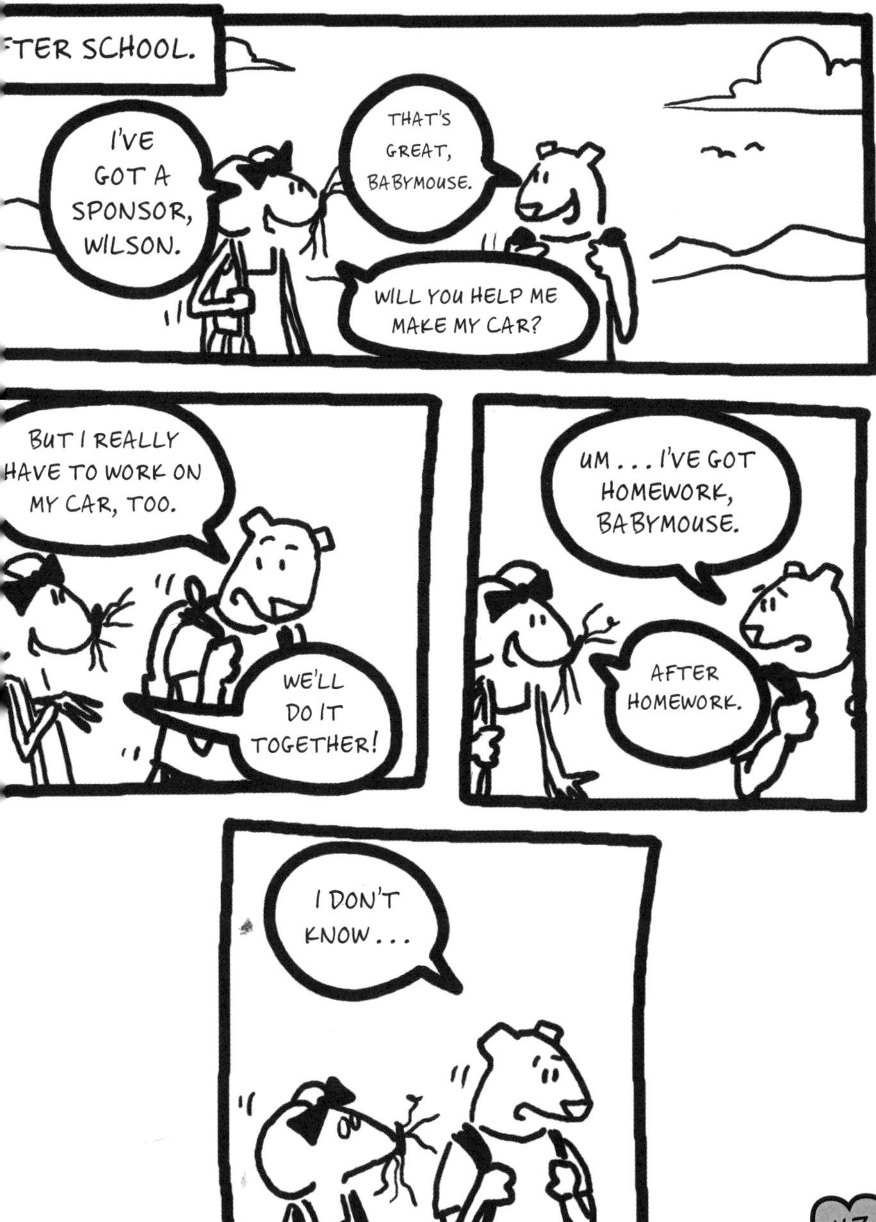

TER SCHOOL.
I'VE GOT A SPONSOR, WILSON.
THAT'S GREAT, BABYMOUSE.
WILL YOU HELP ME MAKE MY CAR?
BUT I REALLY HAVE TO WORK ON MY CAR, TOO.
WE'LL DO IT TOGETHER!
UM . . . I'VE GOT HOMEWORK, BABYMOUSE.
AFTER HOMEWORK.
I DON'T KNOW . . .

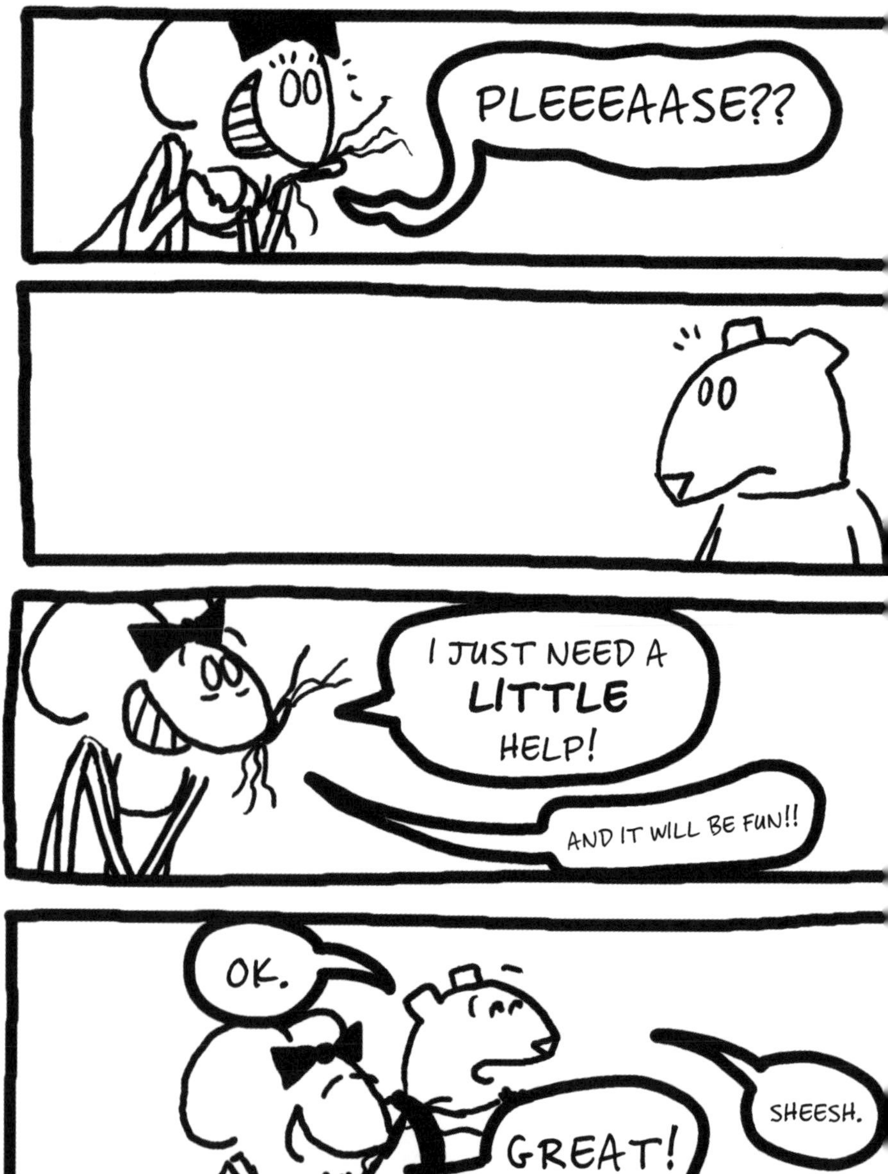
PLEEEAASE??
I JUST NEED A LITTLE HELP!
AND IT WILL BE FUN!!
OK.
GREAT!
SHEESH.

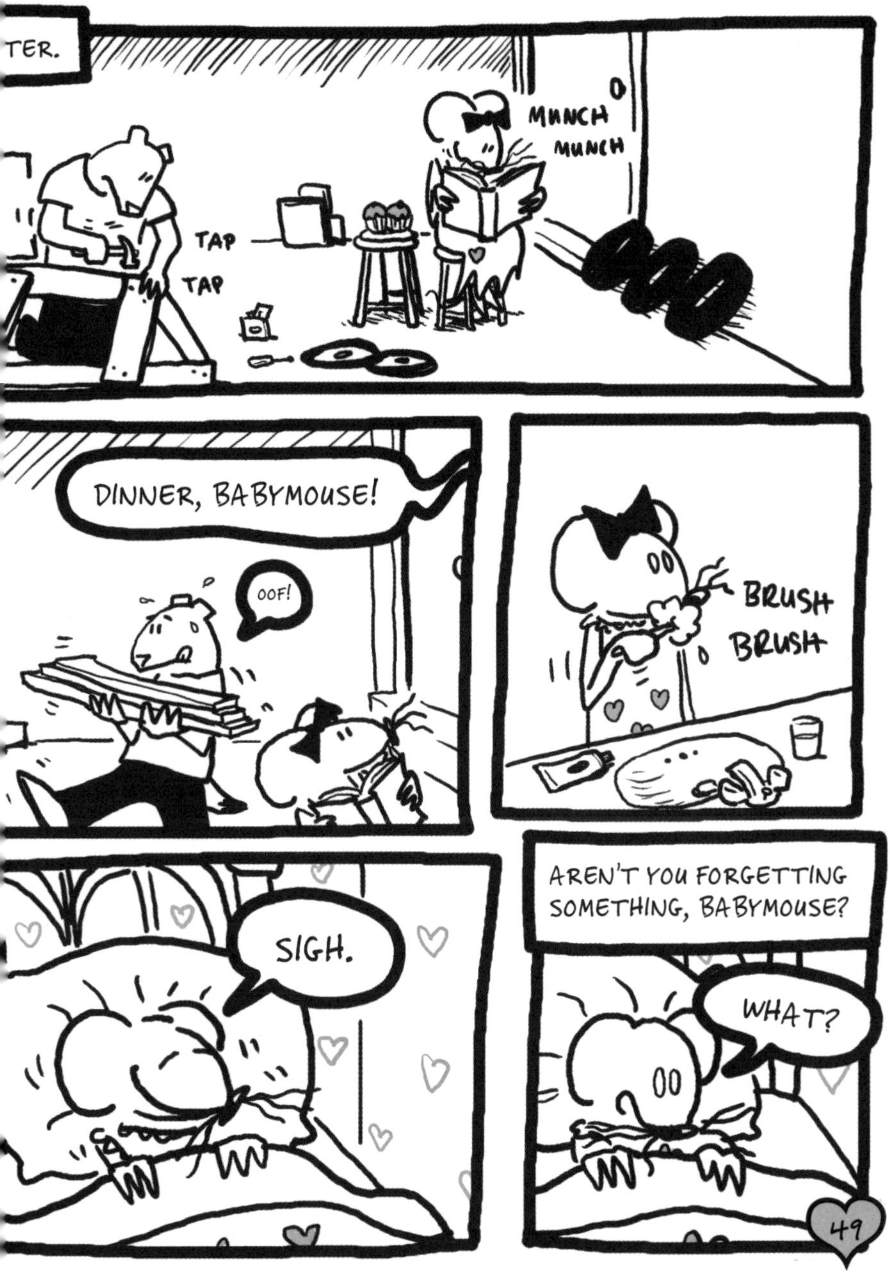

TER.
TAP
TAP
MUNCH
MUNCH
DINNER, BABYMOUSE!
OOF!
BRUSH
BRUSH
SIGH.
AREN'T YOU FORGETTING SOMETHING, BABYMOUSE?
WHAT?

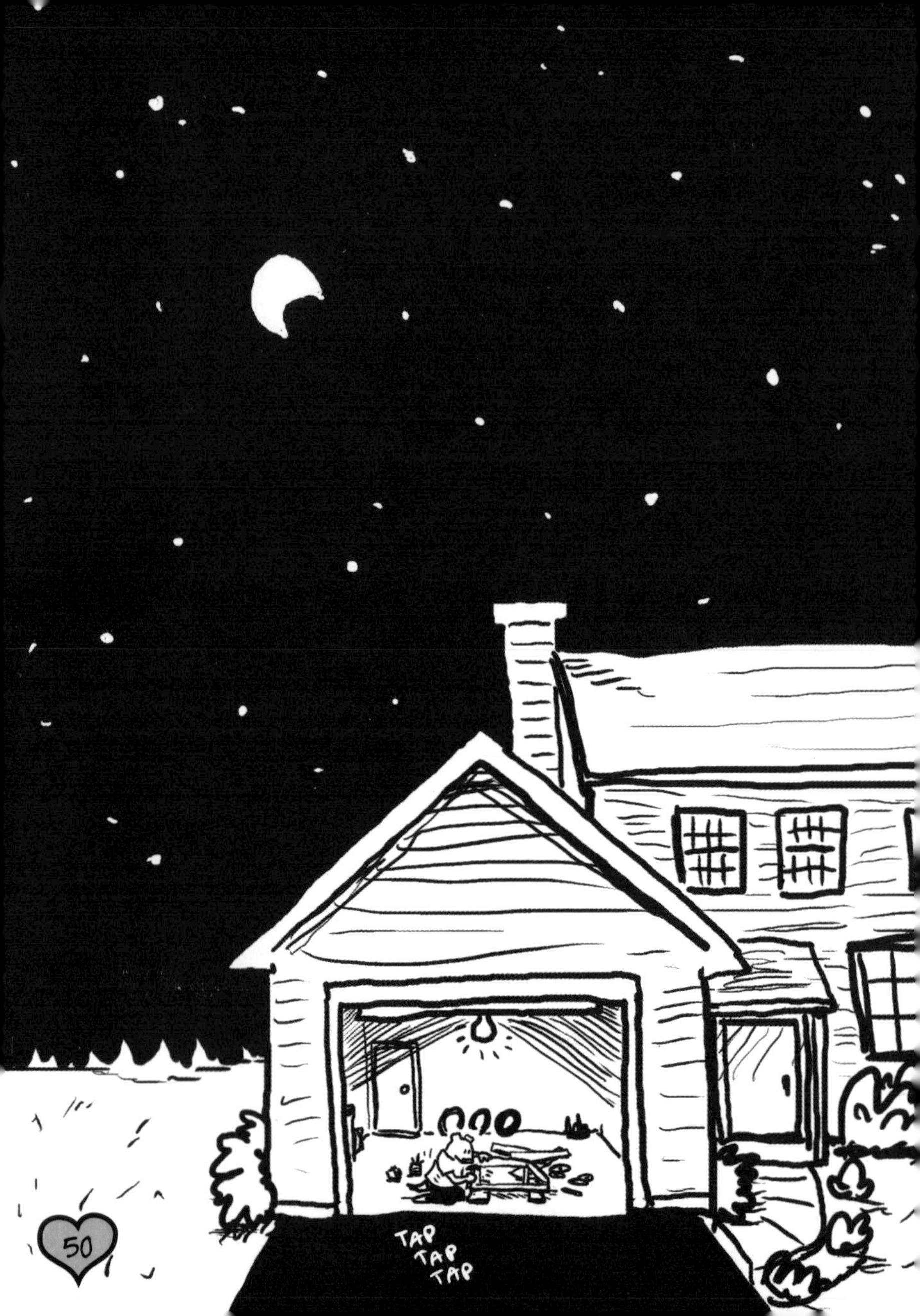
TAP
TAP
TAP

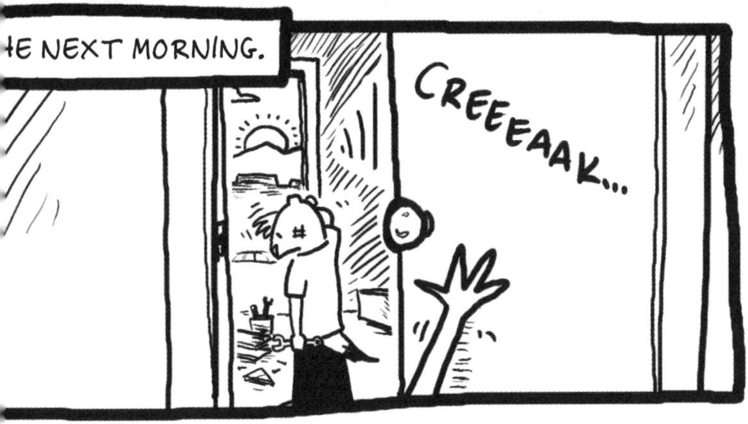
HE NEXT MORNING.
CREEEEAAAK...

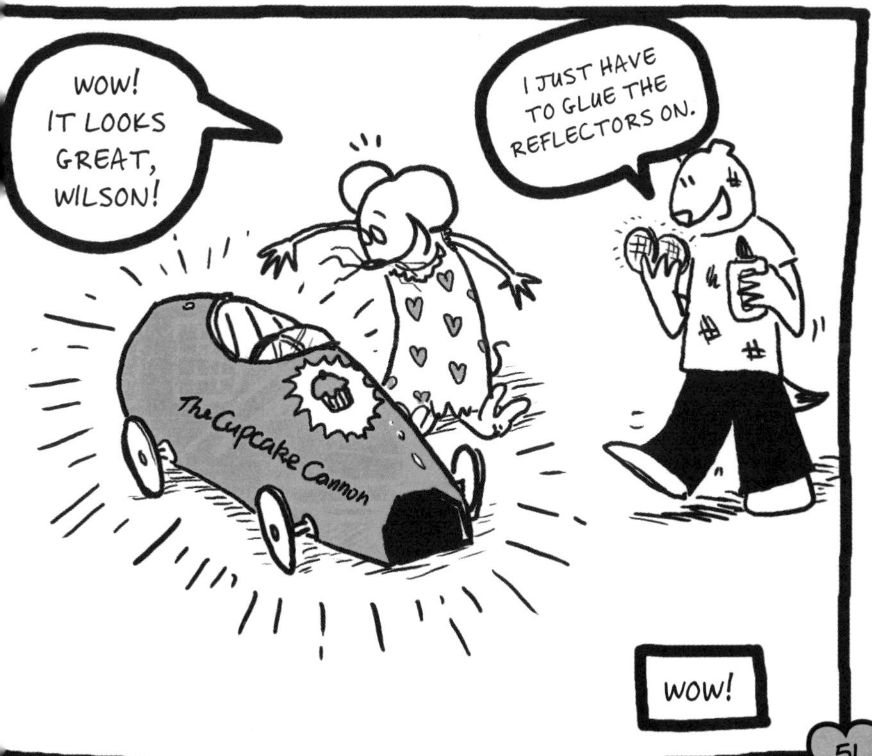
WOW! IT LOOKS GREAT, WILSON!
I JUST HAVE TO GLUE THE REFLECTORS ON.
The Cupcake Cannon
WOW!

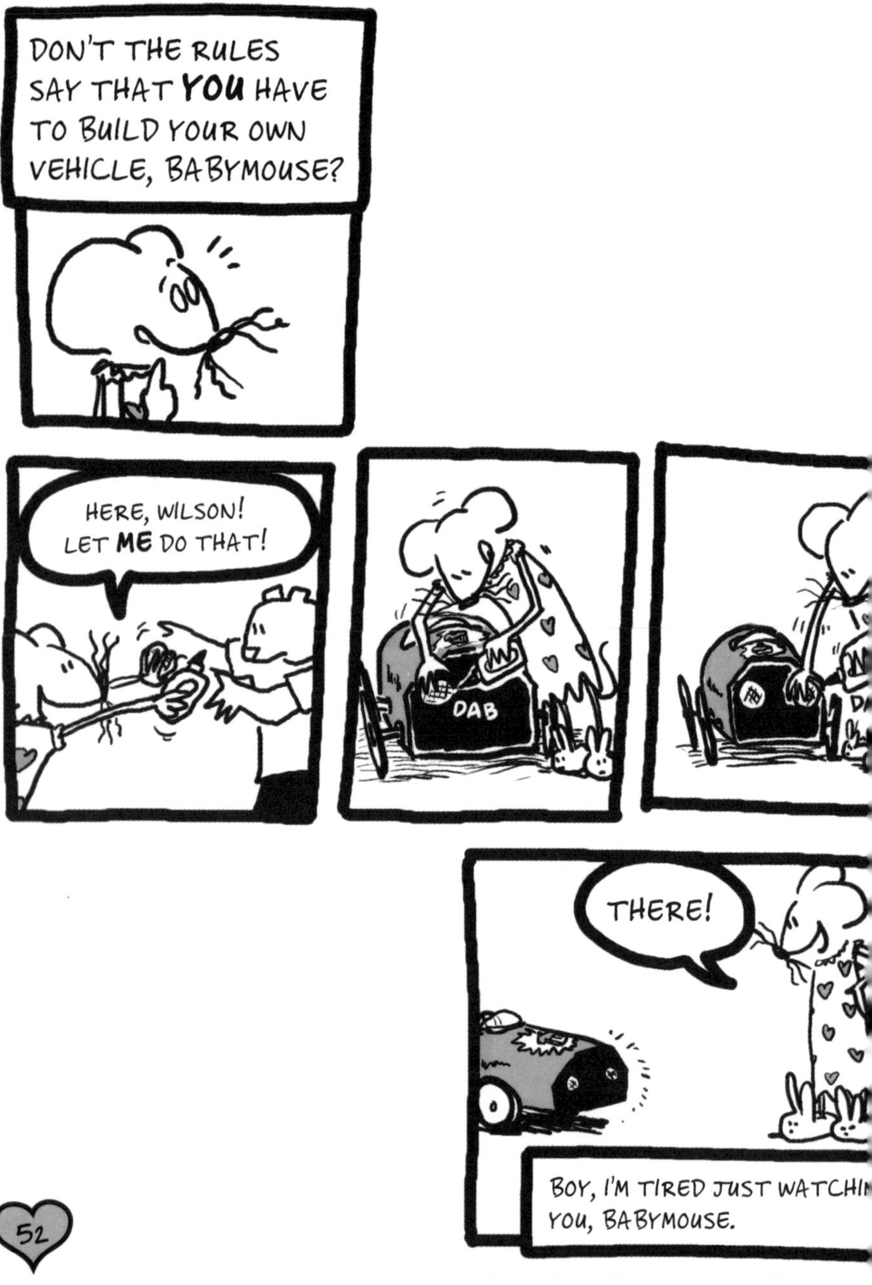
DON'T THE RULES SAY THAT **YOU** HAVE TO BUILD YOUR OWN VEHICLE, BABYMOUSE?
HERE, WILSON! LET **ME** DO THAT!
DAB
THERE!
BOY, I'M TIRED JUST WATCHI
YOU, BABYMOUSE.

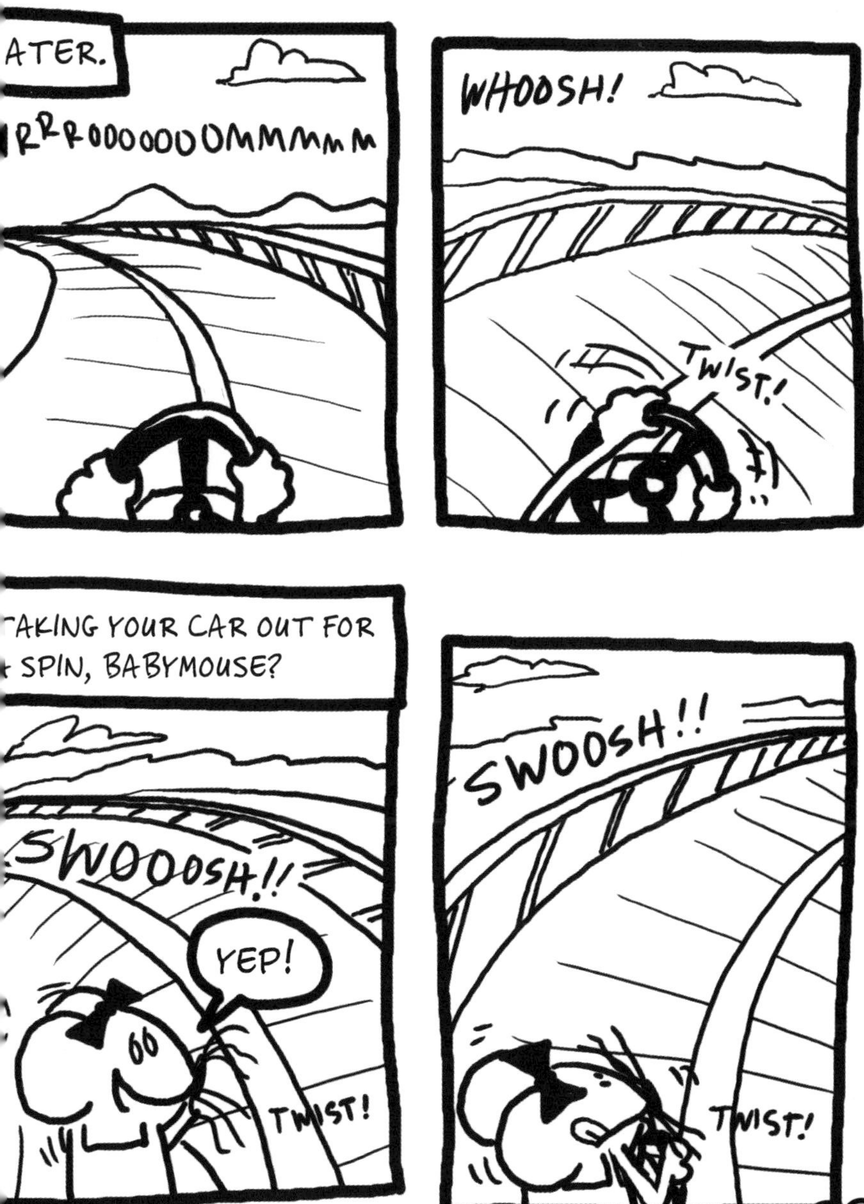
ATER.
RRROOOOOOOOMMMMMM
WHOOSH!
TWIST!
TAKING YOUR CAR OUT FOR
SPIN, BABYMOUSE?
SWOOOSH!!
YEP!
TWIST!
SWOOSH!!
TWIST!

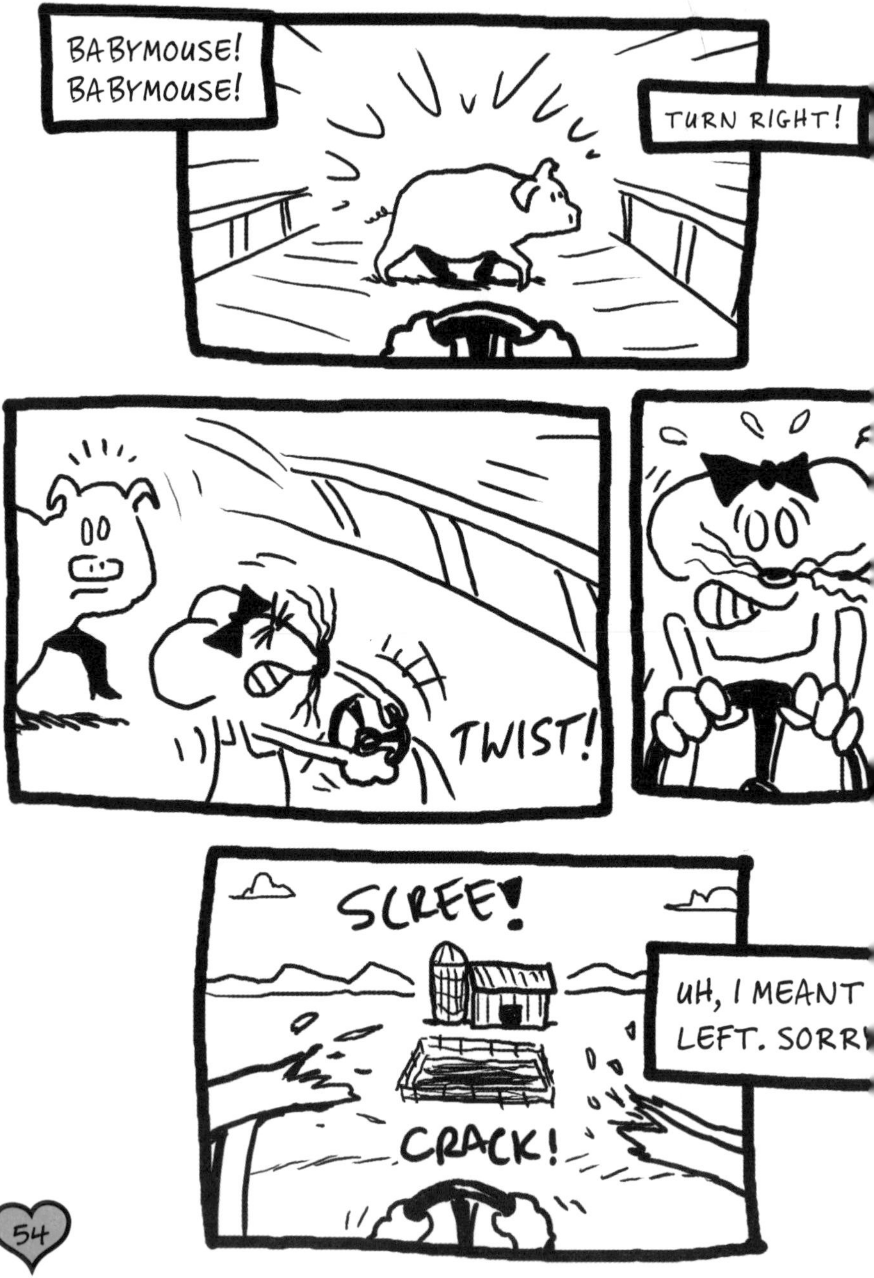
BABYMOUSE! BABYMOUSE!
TURN RIGHT!
TWIST!
SCREE!
CRACK!
UH, I MEANT LEFT. SORR

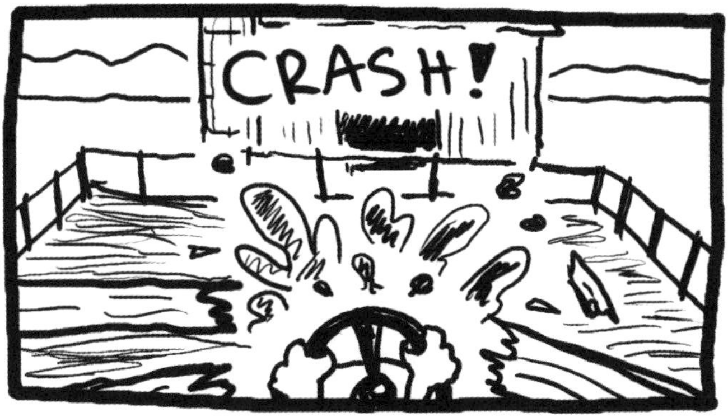
CRASH!

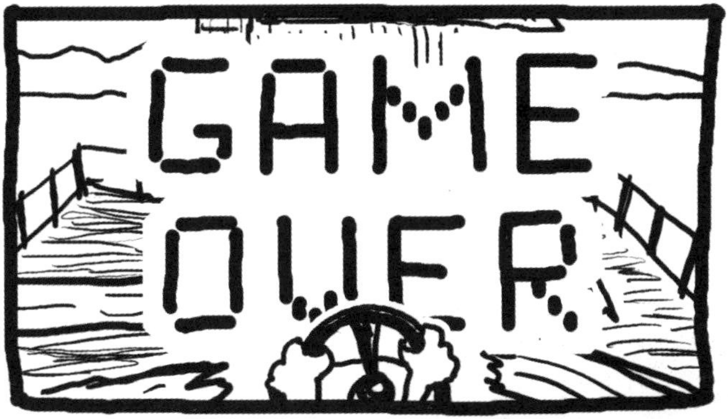
GAME OVER

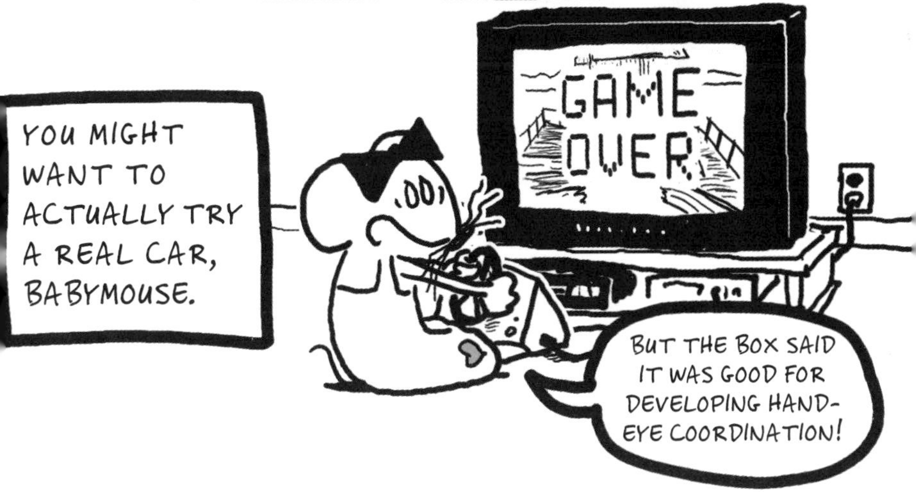
YOU MIGHT WANT TO ACTUALLY TRY A REAL CAR, BABYMOUSE.
GAME OVER
BUT THE BOX SAID IT WAS GOOD FOR DEVELOPING HAND-EYE COORDINATION!

THE NEXT DAY.
SOAP BOX DERBY PRACTICE COURSE
The Cupcake Cannon
TRUDGE
TRUDGE
BABYMOUSE
DOWN!

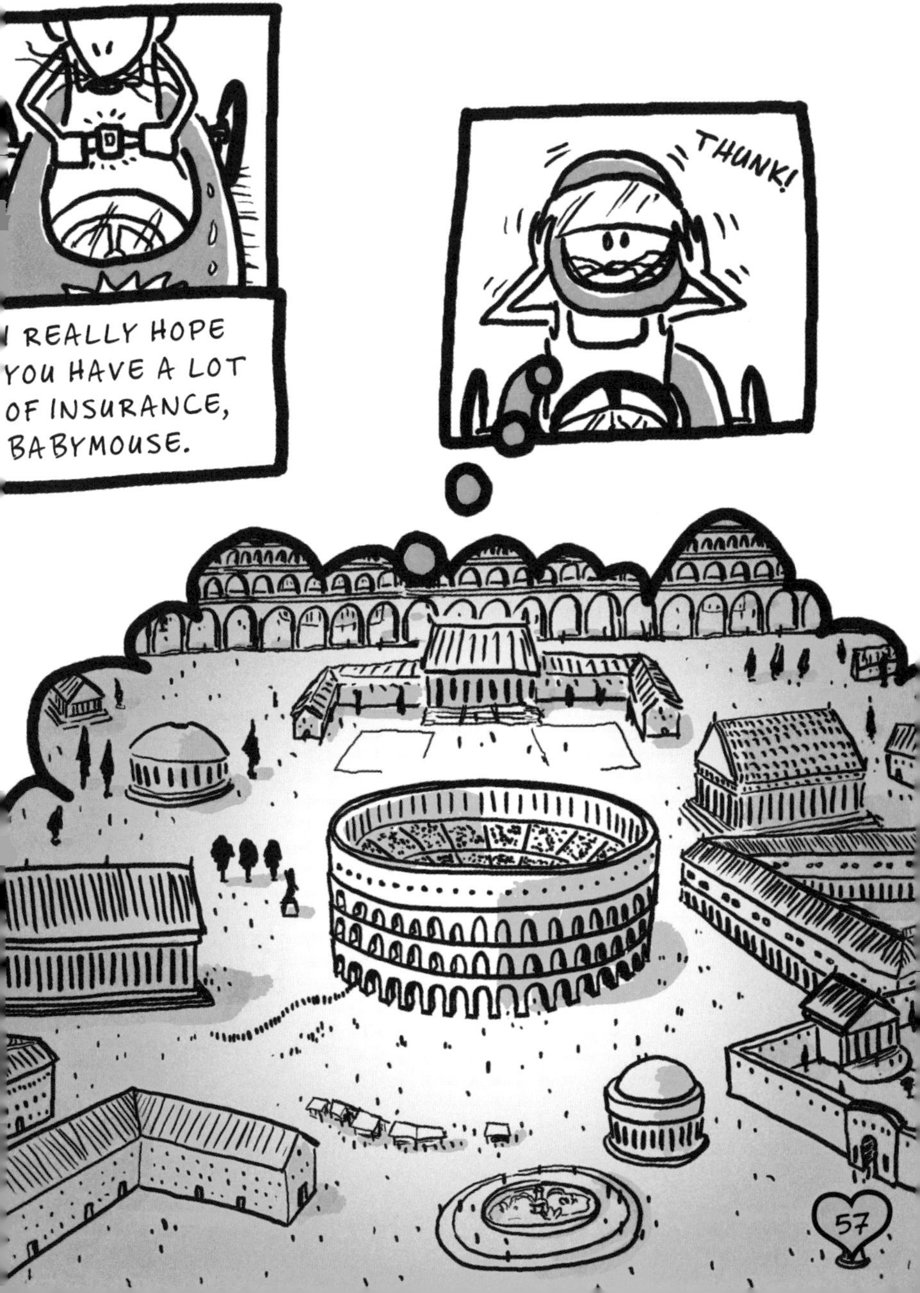
I REALLY HOPE YOU HAVE A LOT OF INSURANCE, BABYMOUSE.
THUNK!

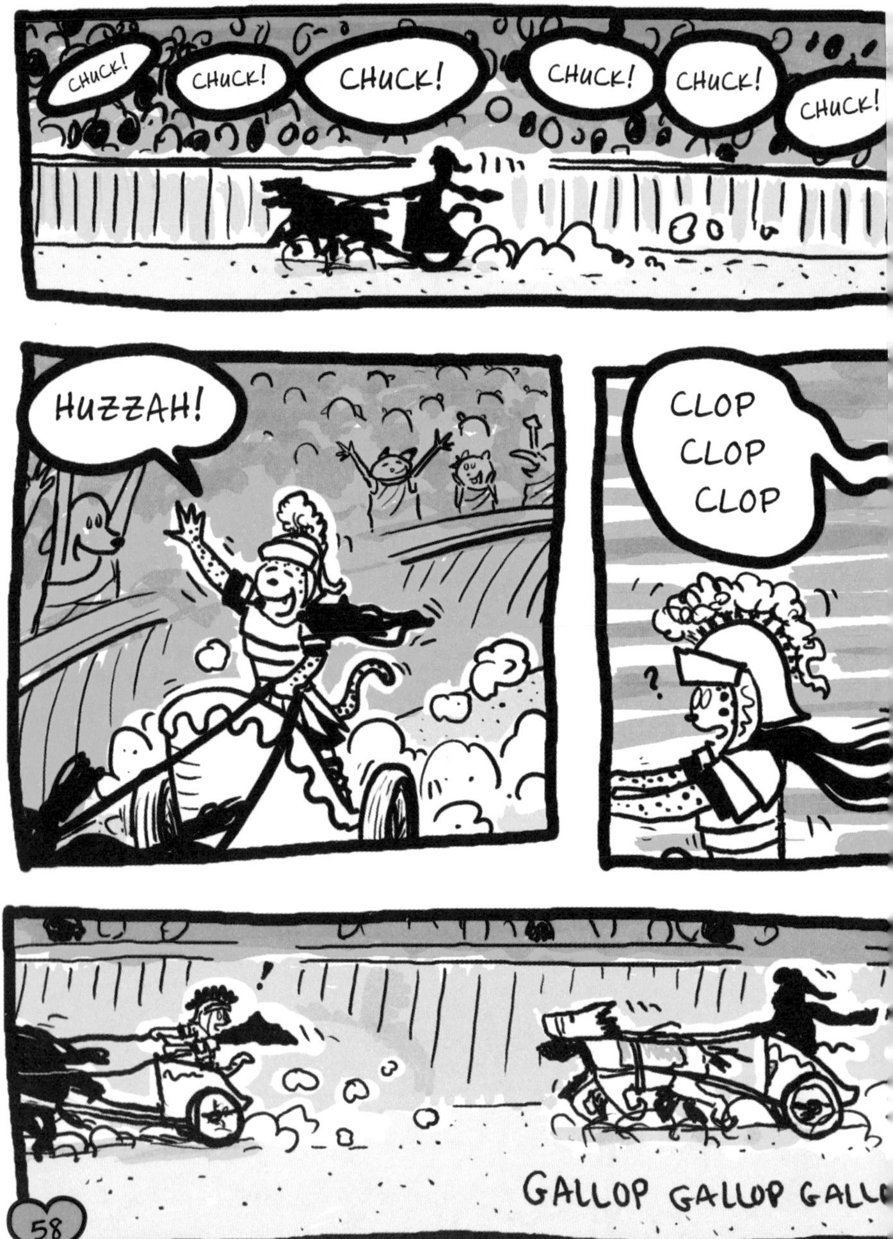
CHUCK!
CHUCK!
CHUCK!
CHUCK!
CHUCK!
CHUCK!
HUZZAH!
CLOP CLOP CLOP
?
!
GALLOP GALLOP GALL

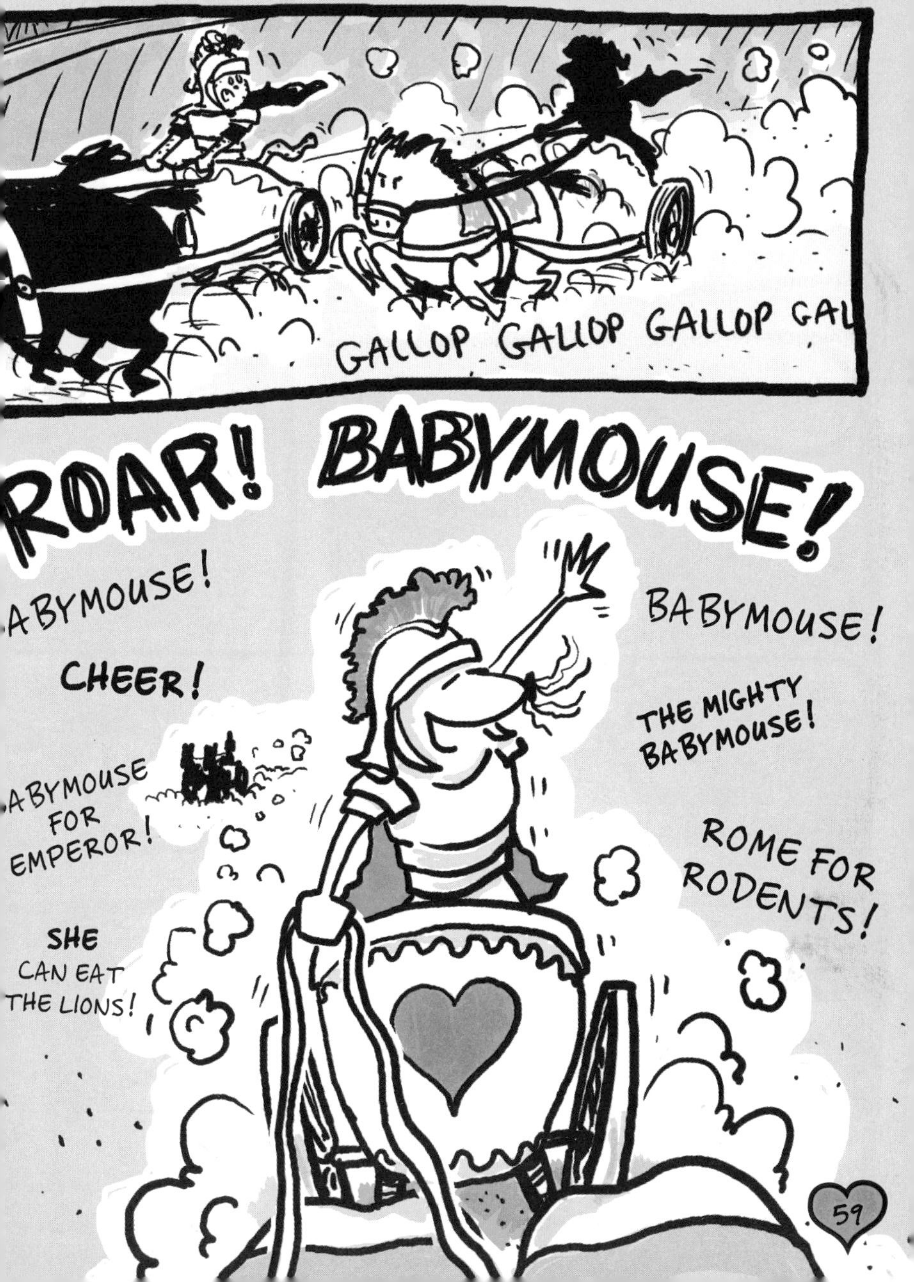

GALLOP GALLOP GALLOP GAL
ROAR! BABYMOUSE!
ABYMOUSE!
BABYMOUSE!
CHEER!
THE MIGHTY BABYMOUSE!
ABYMOUSE FOR EMPEROR!
ROME FOR RODENTS!
SHE CAN EAT THE LIONS!

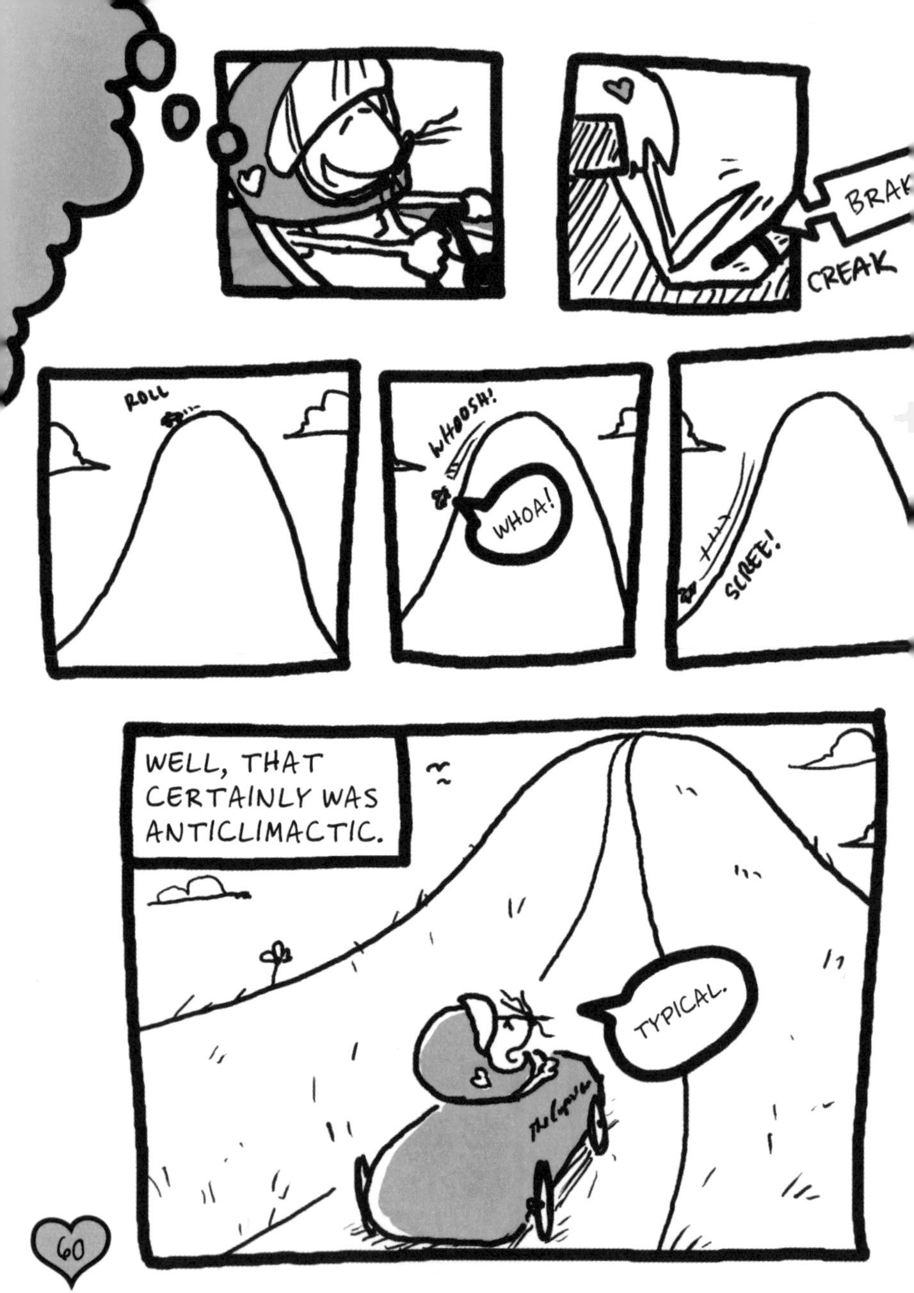
BRAK
CREAK
ROLL
WHOOSH!
WHOA!
SCREE!
WELL, THAT CERTAINLY WAS ANTICLIMACTIC.
TYPICAL.

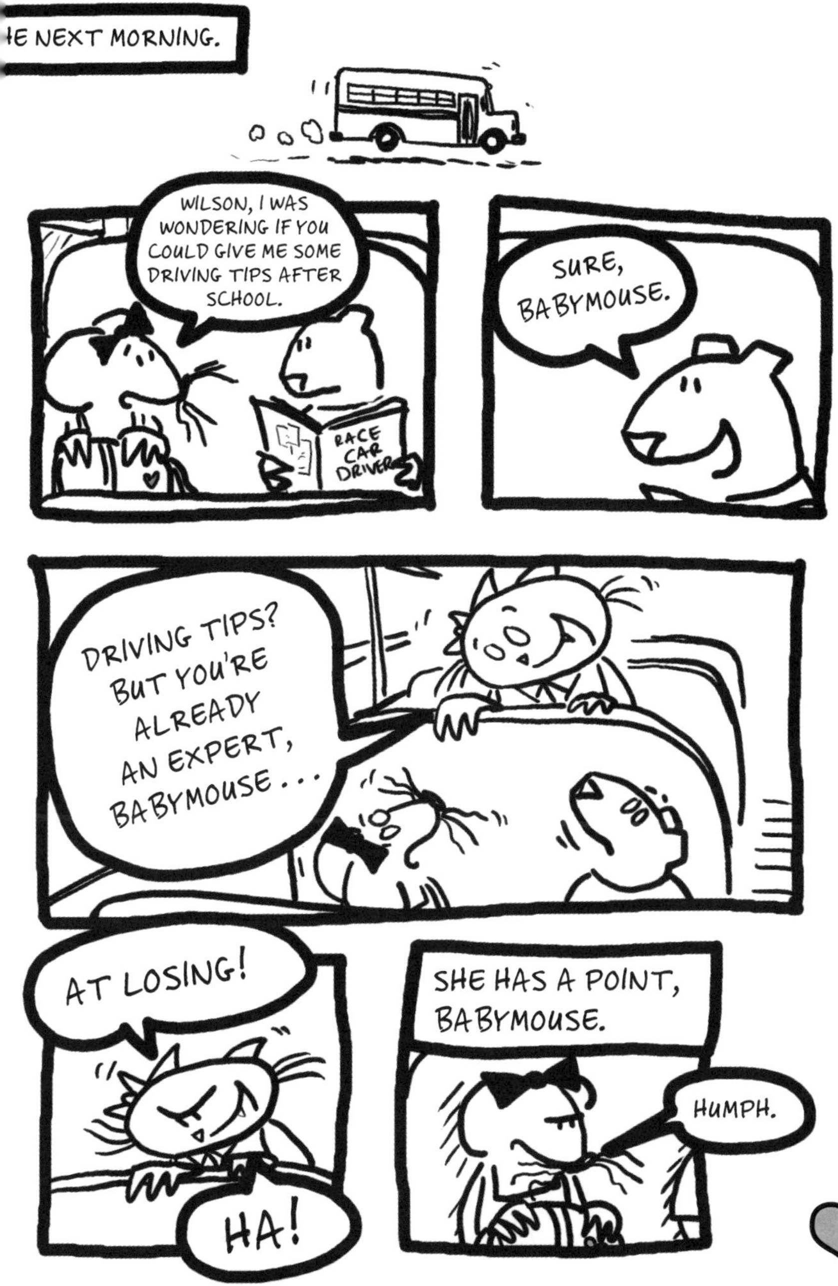

HE NEXT MORNING.
WILSON, I WAS WONDERING IF YOU COULD GIVE ME SOME DRIVING TIPS AFTER SCHOOL.
RACE CAR DRIVER
SURE, BABYMOUSE.
DRIVING TIPS? BUT YOU'RE ALREADY AN EXPERT, BABYMOUSE . . .
AT LOSING!
HA!
SHE HAS A POINT, BABYMOUSE.
HUMPH.

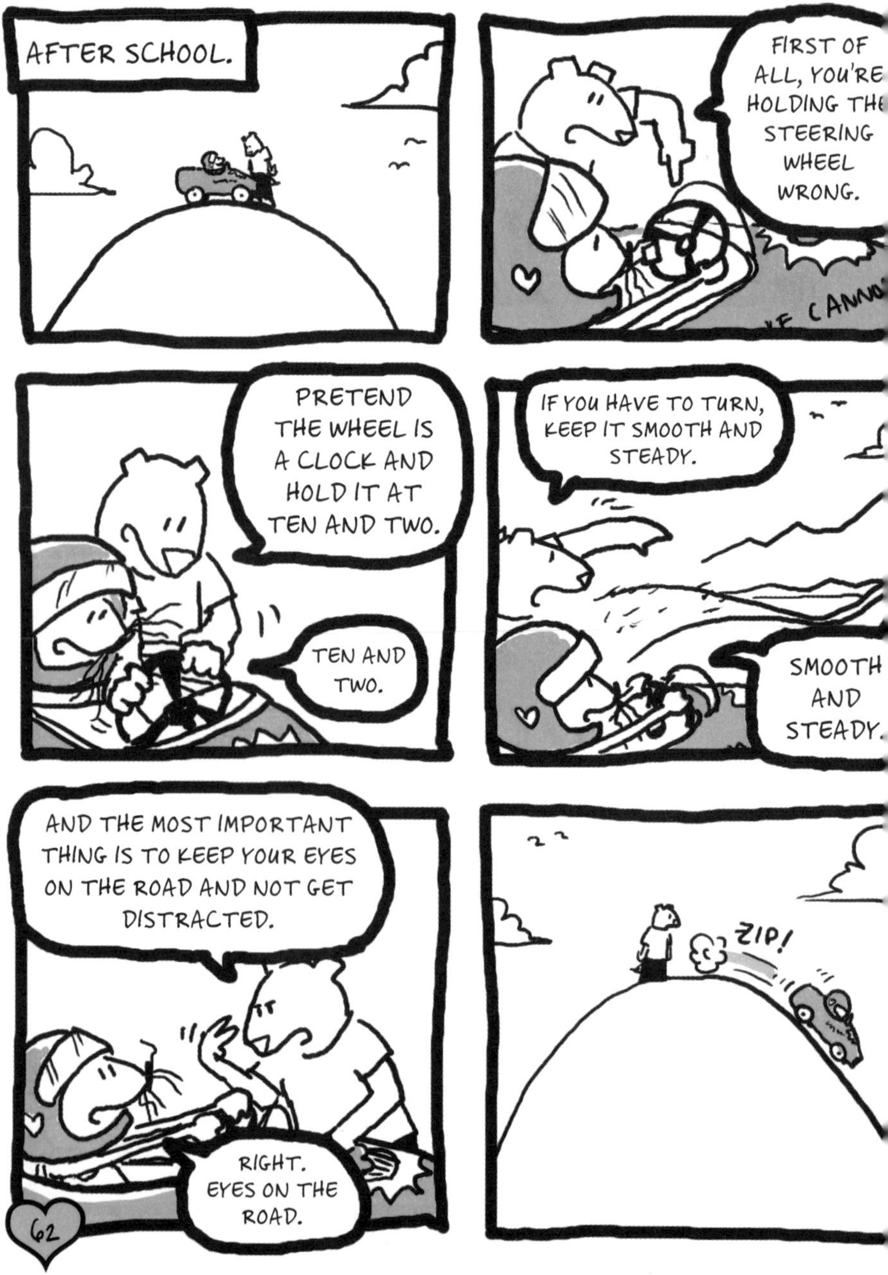
AFTER SCHOOL.
FIRST OF ALL, YOU'RE HOLDING THE STEERING WHEEL WRONG.
PRETEND THE WHEEL IS A CLOCK AND HOLD IT AT TEN AND TWO.
TEN AND TWO.
IF YOU HAVE TO TURN, KEEP IT SMOOTH AND STEADY.
SMOOTH AND STEADY.
AND THE MOST IMPORTANT THING IS TO KEEP YOUR EYES ON THE ROAD AND NOT GET DISTRACTED.
RIGHT. EYES ON THE ROAD.
ZIP!

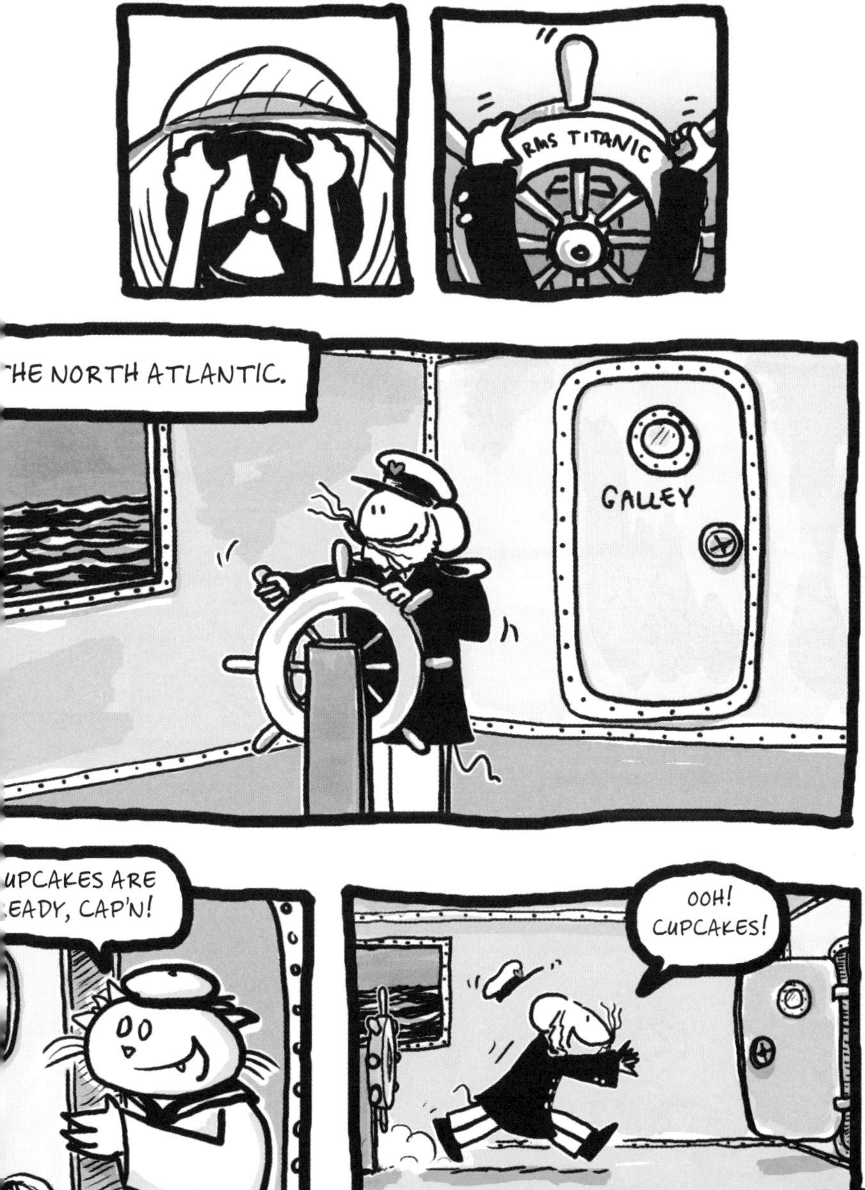
RMS TITANIC
HE NORTH ATLANTIC.
GALLEY
UPCAKES ARE EADY, CAP'N!
OOH! CUPCAKES!

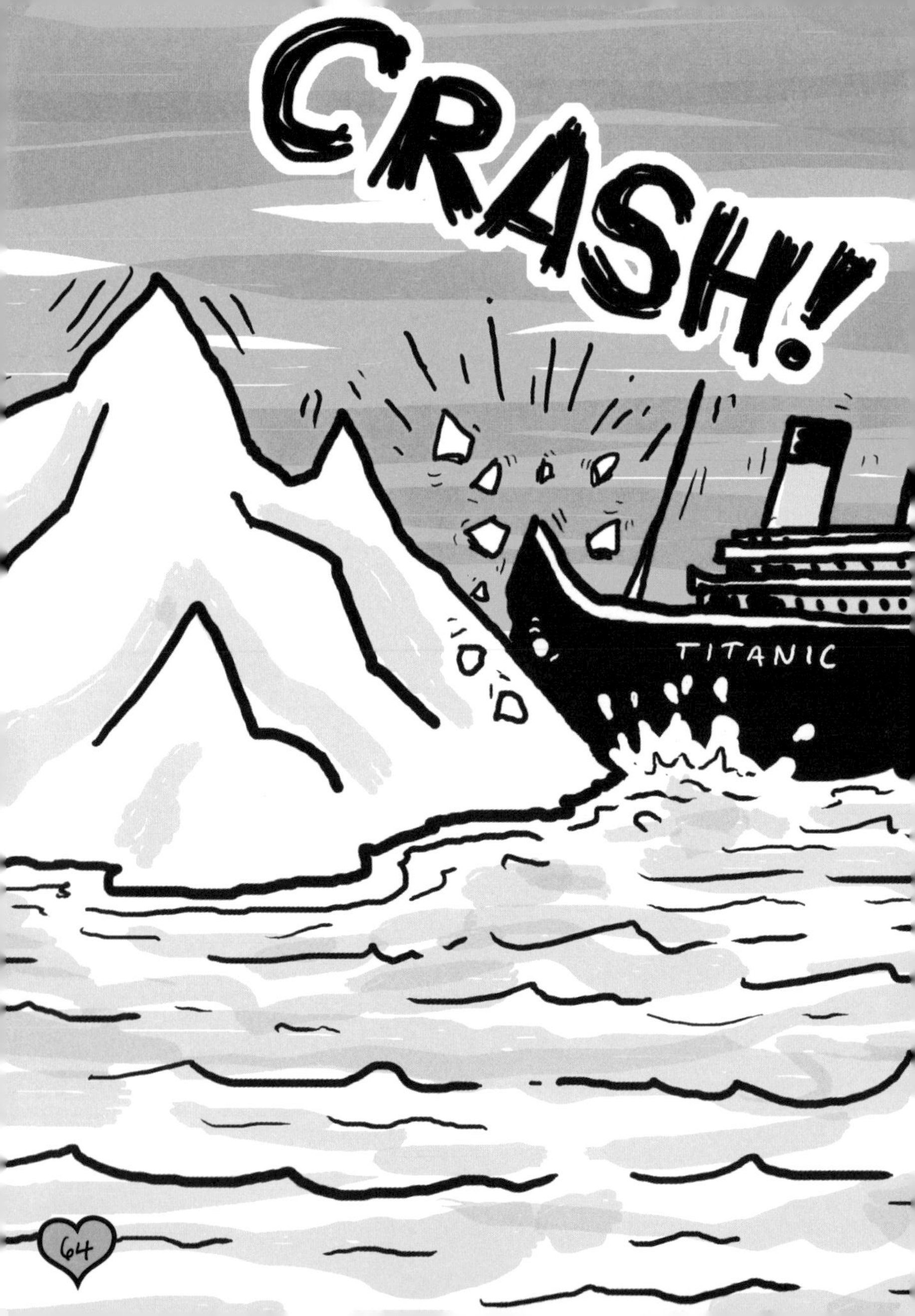
CRASH!
TITANIC

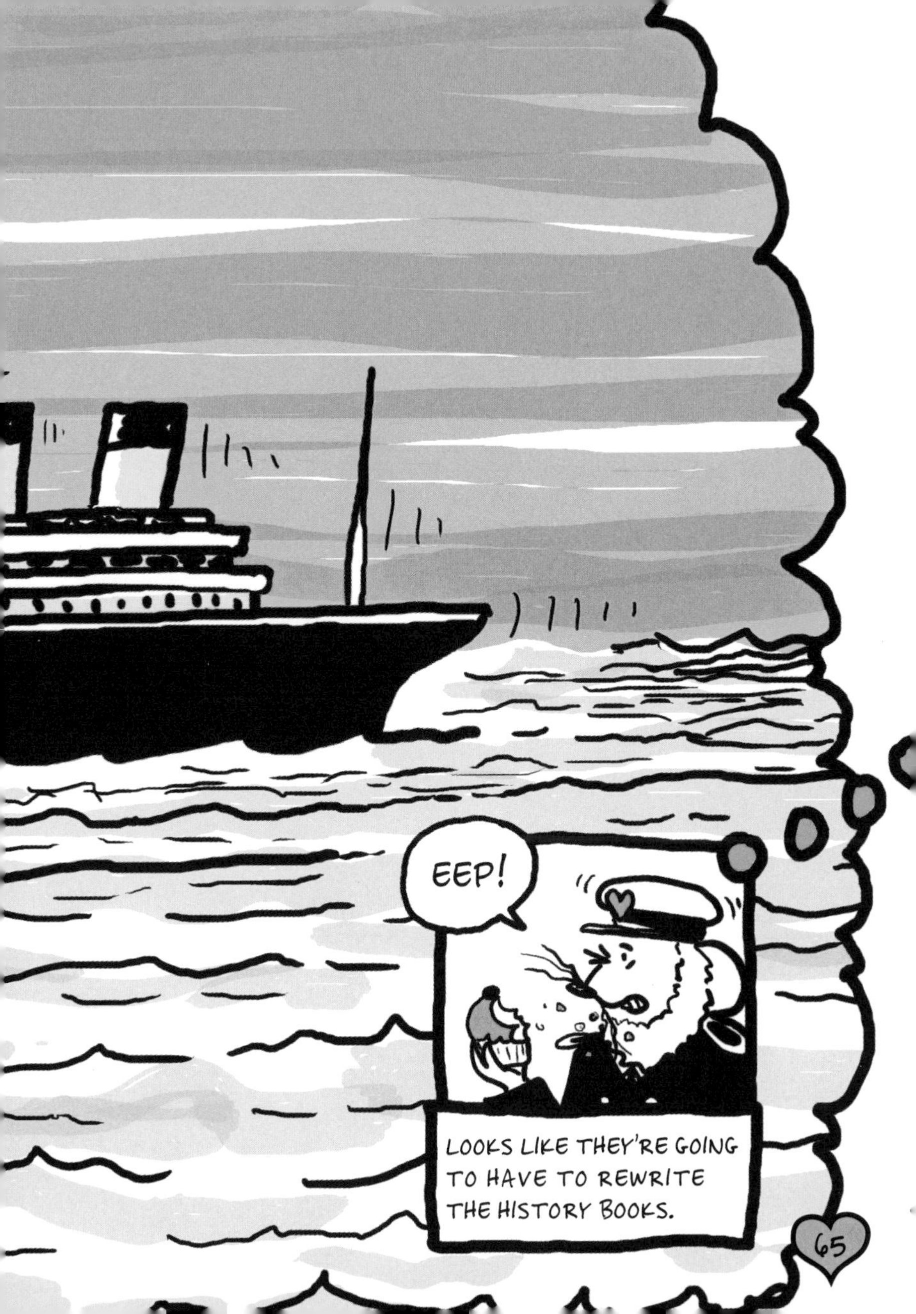
EEP!
LOOKS LIKE THEY'RE GOING TO HAVE TO REWRITE THE HISTORY BOOKS.

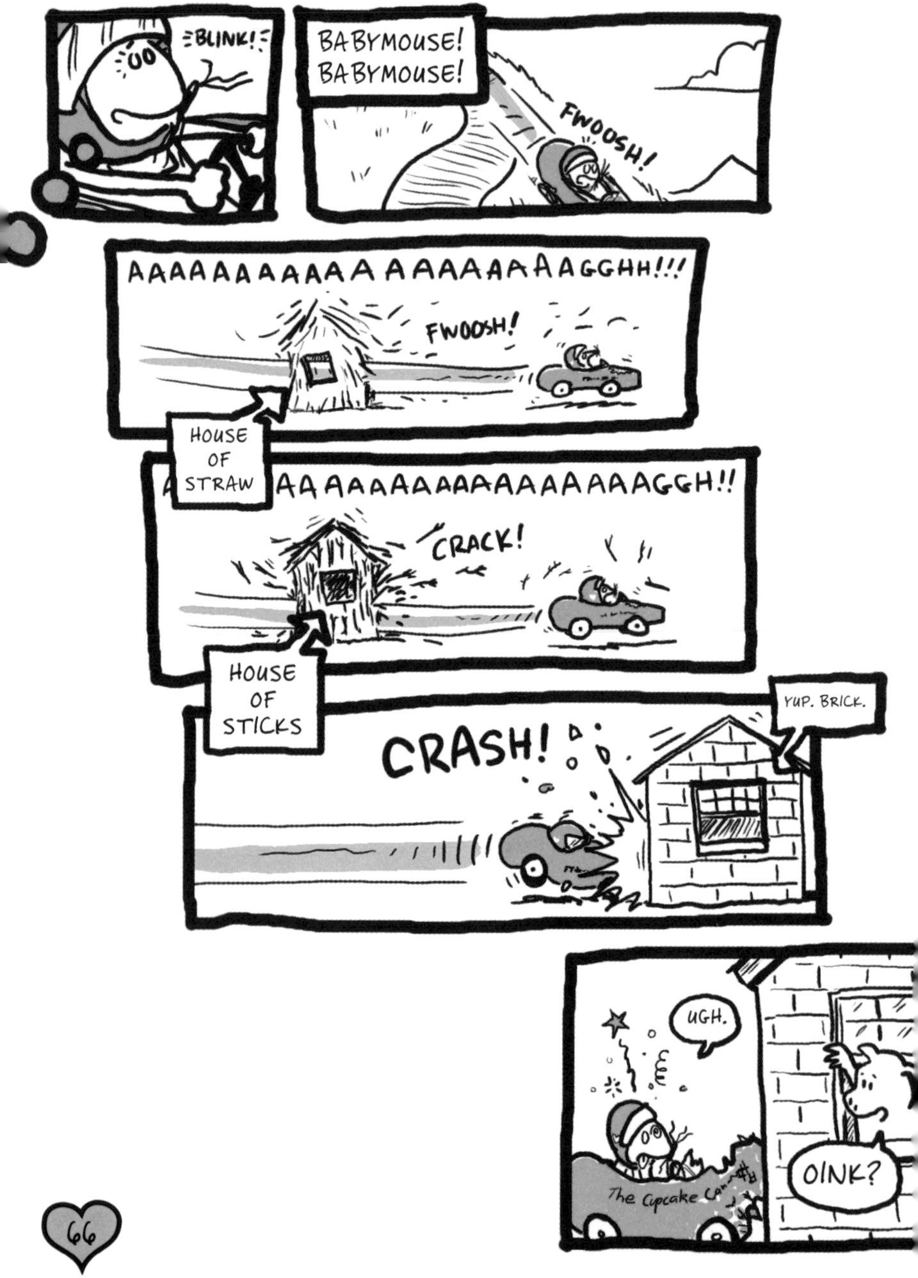
BLINK!
BABYMOUSE! BABYMOUSE!
FWOOSH!
AAAAAAAAAAA AAAAAAAAGGHH!!!
FWOOSH!
HOUSE OF STRAW
AAAAAAAAAAAAAAAAAAAGGH!!
CRACK!
HOUSE OF STICKS
CRASH!
YUP. BRICK.
UGH.
The Cupcake Car
OINK?

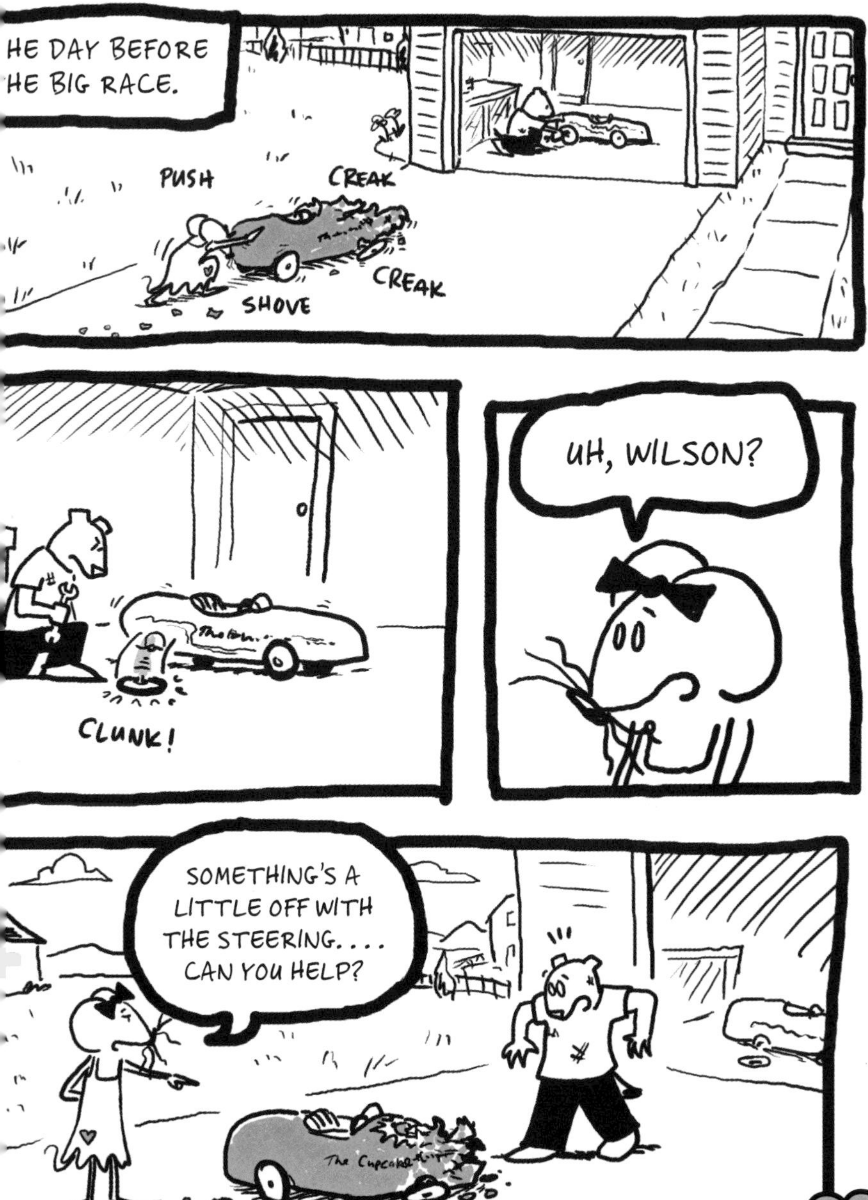
HE DAY BEFORE
HE BIG RACE.
PUSH
CREAK
CREAK
SHOVE
CLUNK!
UH, WILSON?
SOMETHING'S A LITTLE OFF WITH THE STEERING. . . . CAN YOU HELP?

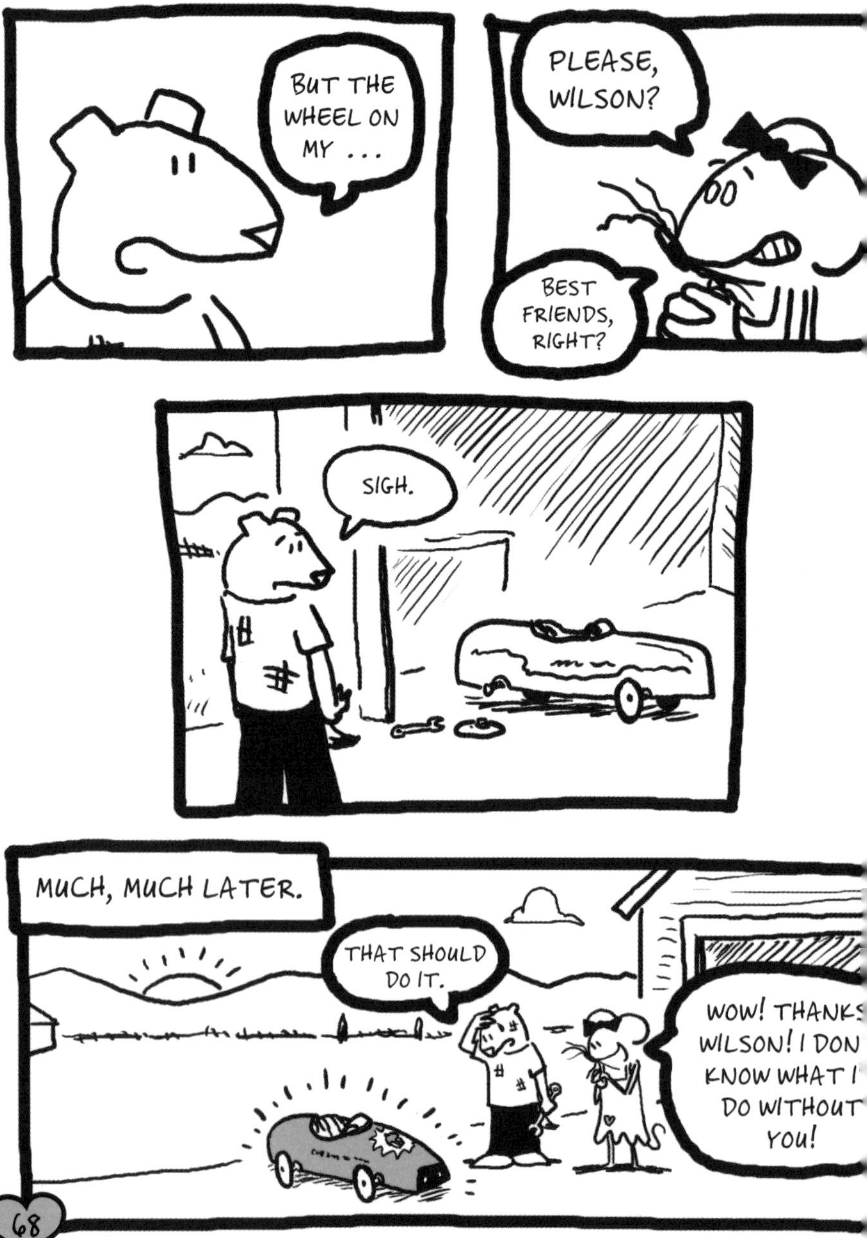
BUT THE WHEEL ON MY ...
PLEASE, WILSON?
BEST FRIENDS, RIGHT?
SIGH.
MUCH, MUCH LATER.
THAT SHOULD DO IT.
WOW! THANKS WILSON! I DON KNOW WHAT I DO WITHOUT YOU!

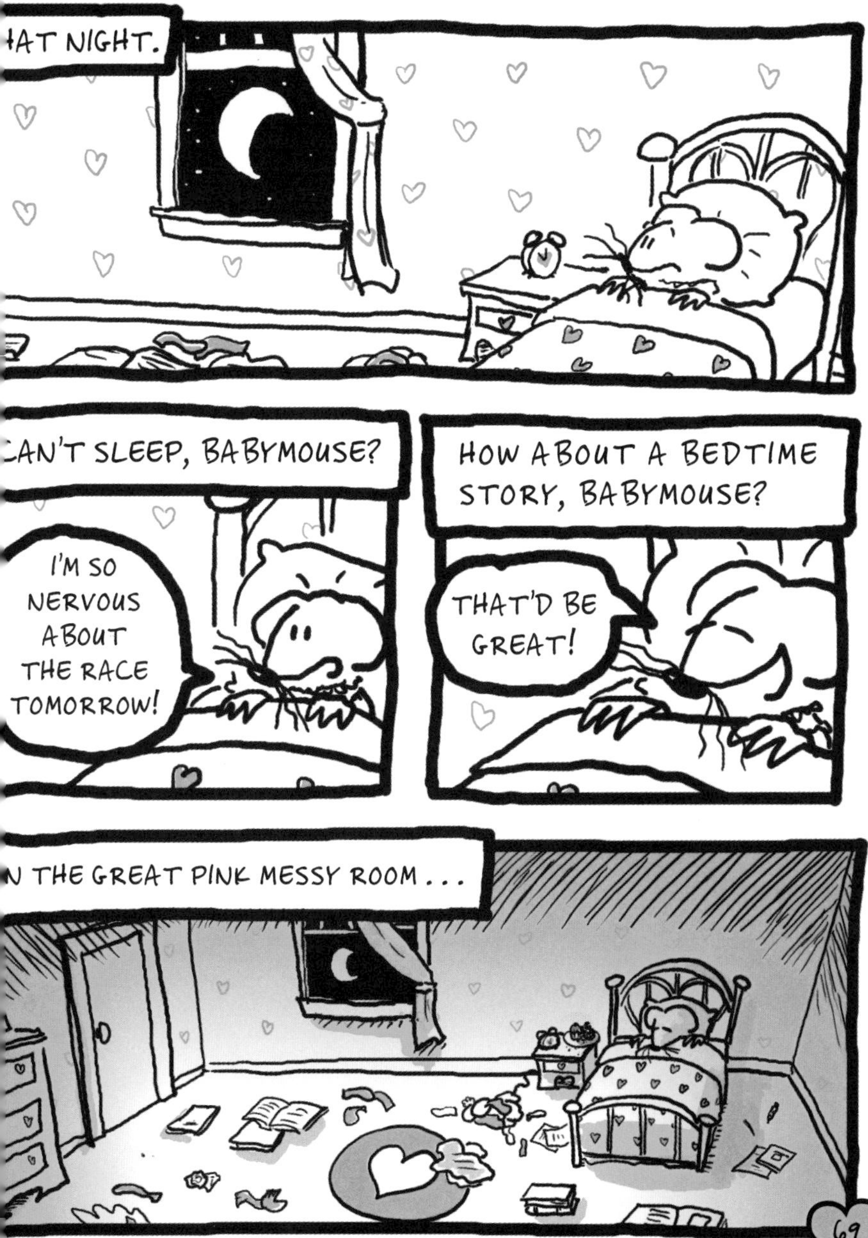
HAT NIGHT.
CAN'T SLEEP, BABYMOUSE?
I'M SO NERVOUS ABOUT THE RACE TOMORROW!
HOW ABOUT A BEDTIME STORY, BABYMOUSE?
THAT'D BE GREAT!
N THE GREAT PINK MESSY ROOM . . .

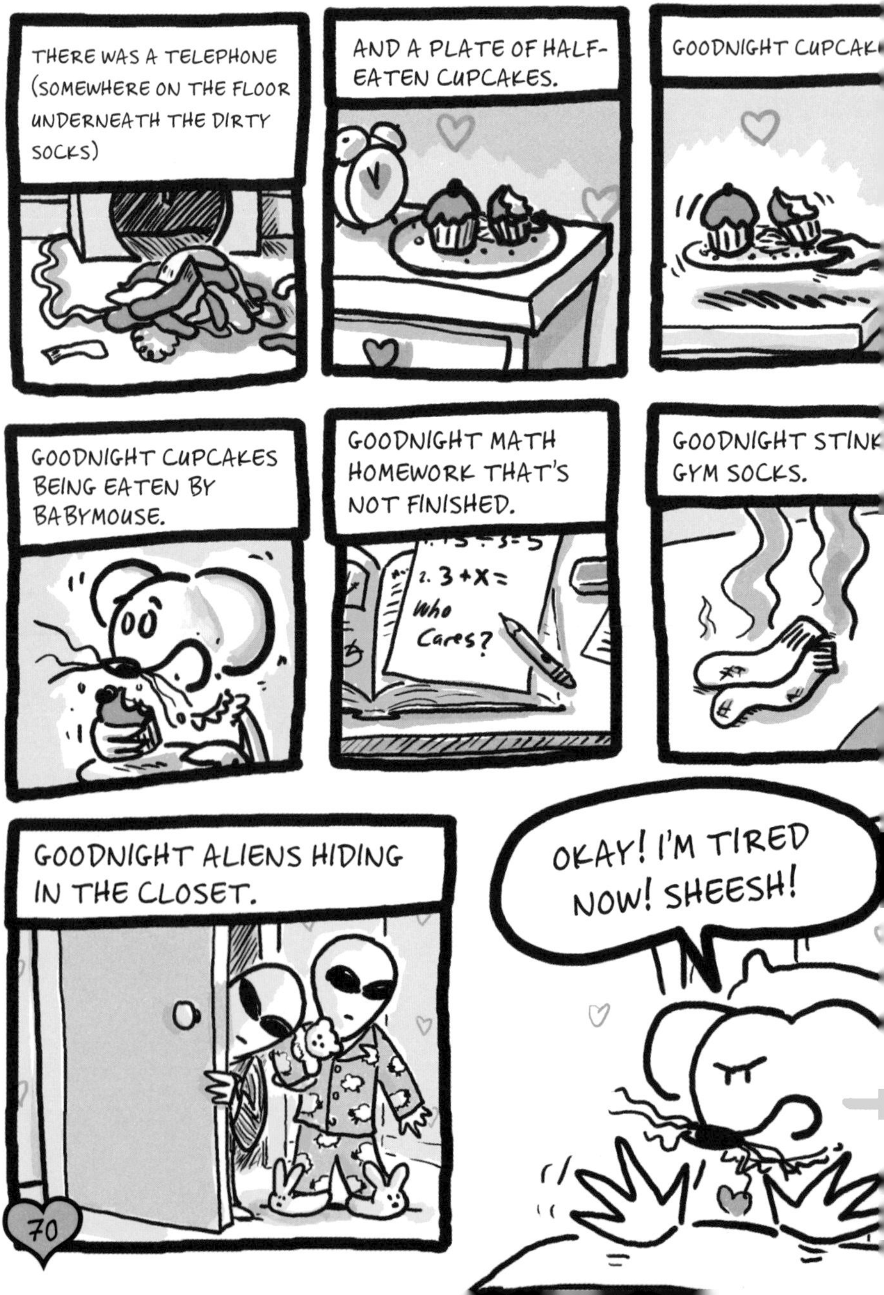
THERE WAS A TELEPHONE (SOMEWHERE ON THE FLOOR UNDERNEATH THE DIRTY SOCKS)
AND A PLATE OF HALF-EATEN CUPCAKES.
GOODNIGHT CUPCAK
GOODNIGHT CUPCAKES BEING EATEN BY BABYMOUSE.
GOODNIGHT MATH HOMEWORK THAT'S NOT FINISHED.
2. 3+X=
Who Cares?
GOODNIGHT STINK GYM SOCKS.
GOODNIGHT ALIENS HIDING IN THE CLOSET.
OKAY! I'M TIRED NOW! SHEESH!

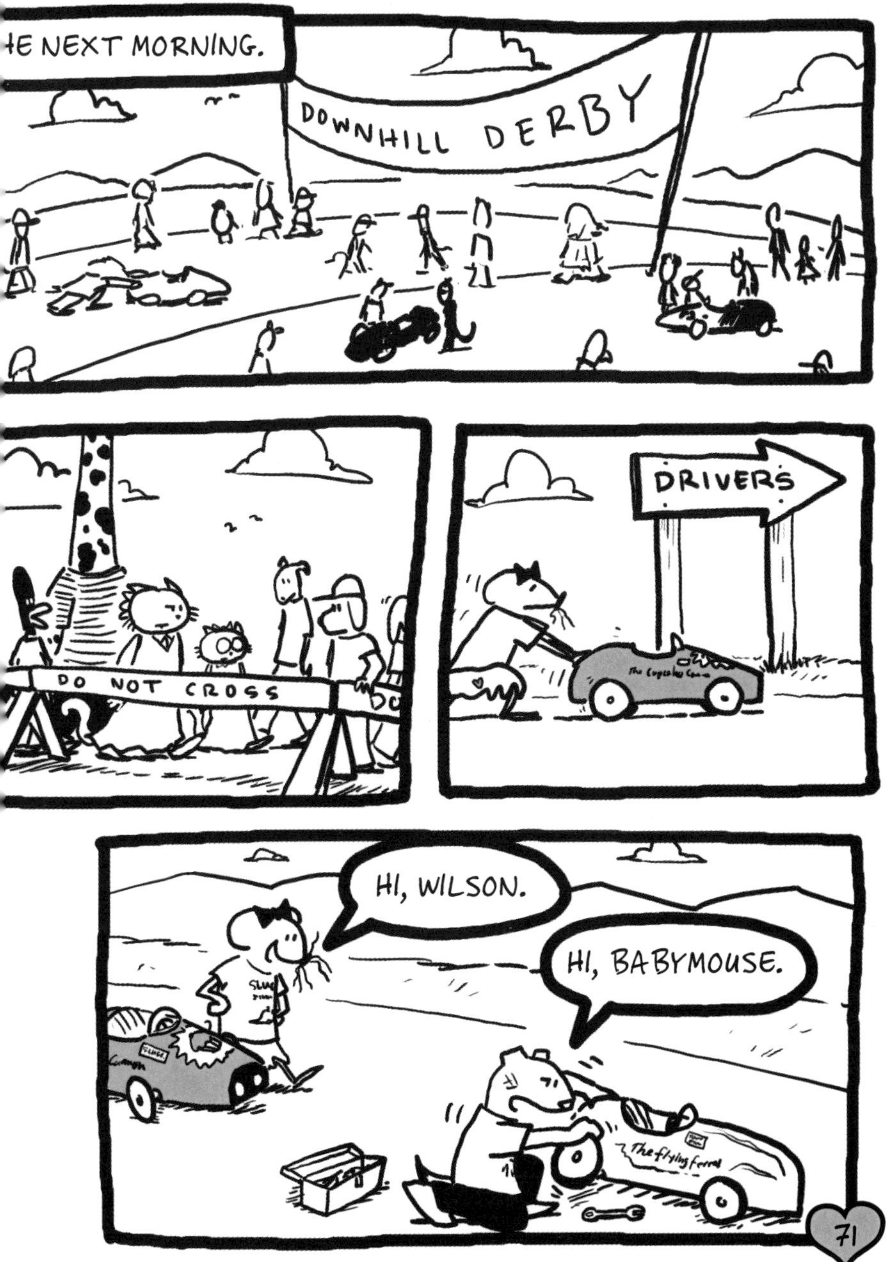
HE NEXT MORNING.
DOWNHILL DERBY
DO NOT CROSS
DRIVERS
HI, WILSON.
HI, BABYMOUSE.
The flying ferret

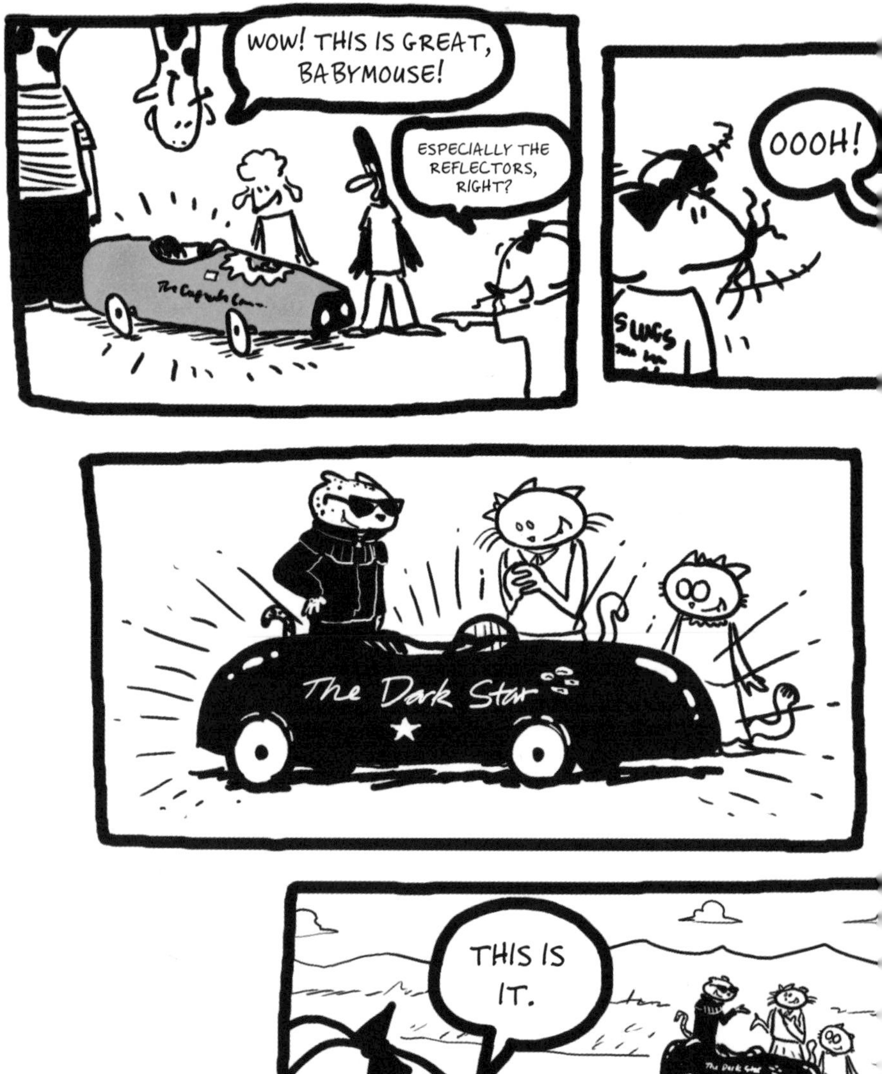
WOW! THIS IS GREAT, BABYMOUSE!
ESPECIALLY THE REFLECTORS, RIGHT?
OOOH!
The Dark Star
THIS IS IT.

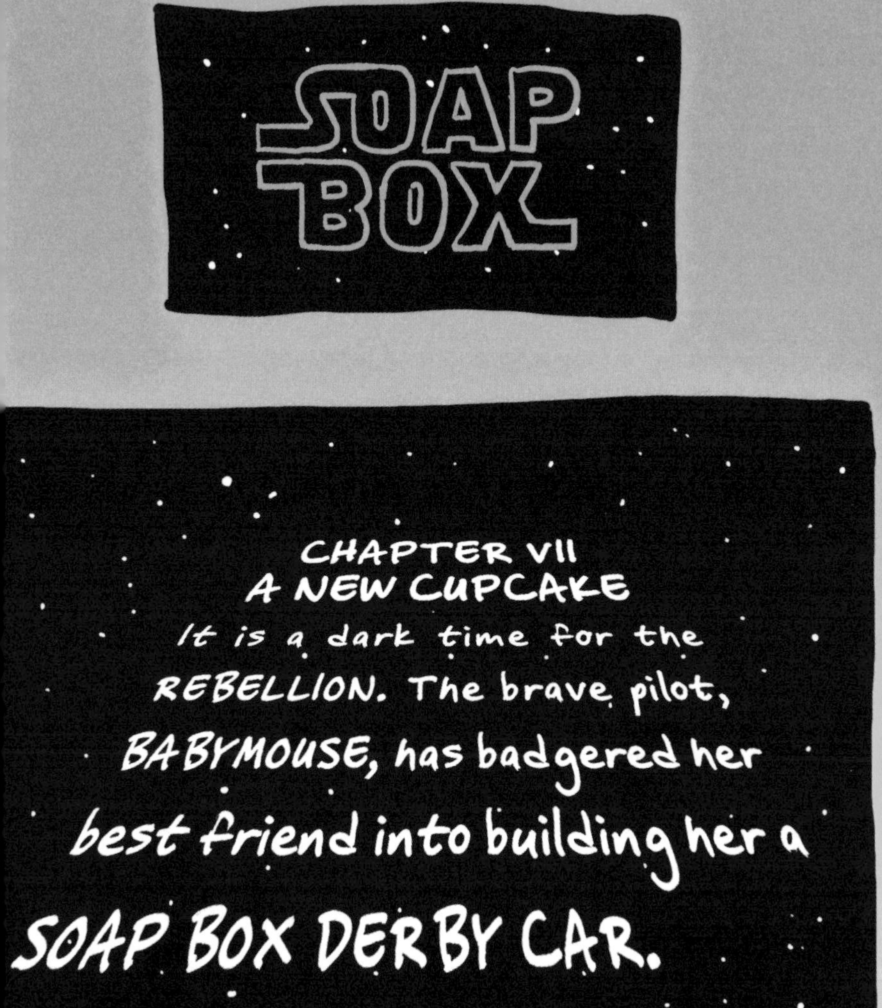
SOAP BOX
CHAPTER VII
A NEW CUPCAKE
It is a dark time for the REBELLION. The brave pilot, BABYMOUSE, has badgered her best friend into building her a SOAP BOX DERBY CAR.

SOAP BOX DERBY CAR.

Little does she know that the villainous CHUCK E. CHEETAH is going to totally mop the floor with her, since he has actually practiced every day for years and she can't avoid crashing into pigpens.

into pigpens.

Now the hour has come at last that will spell certain doom for the blah blah blah blah... are you still reading this?

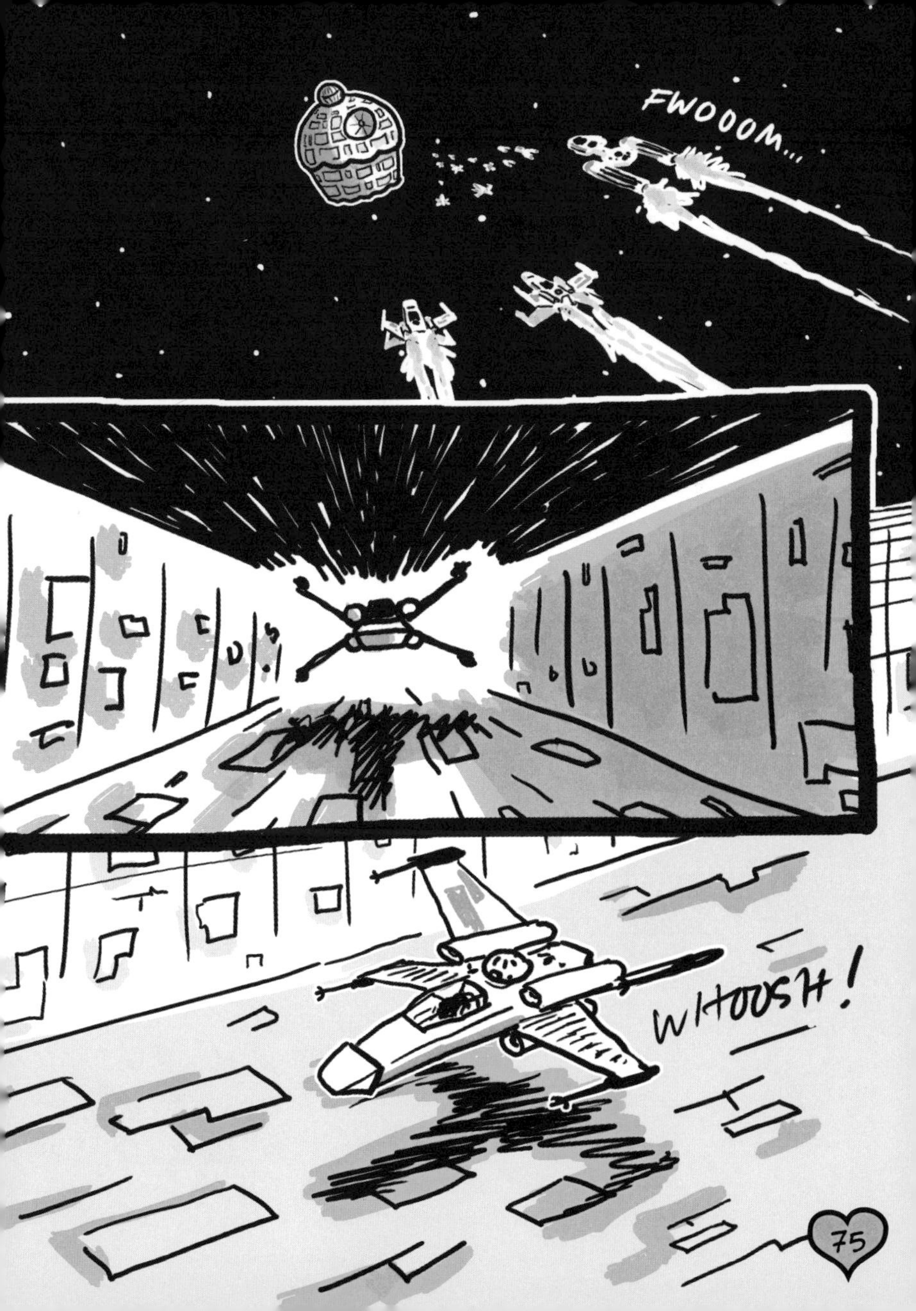
FWOOOM...
WHOOSH!

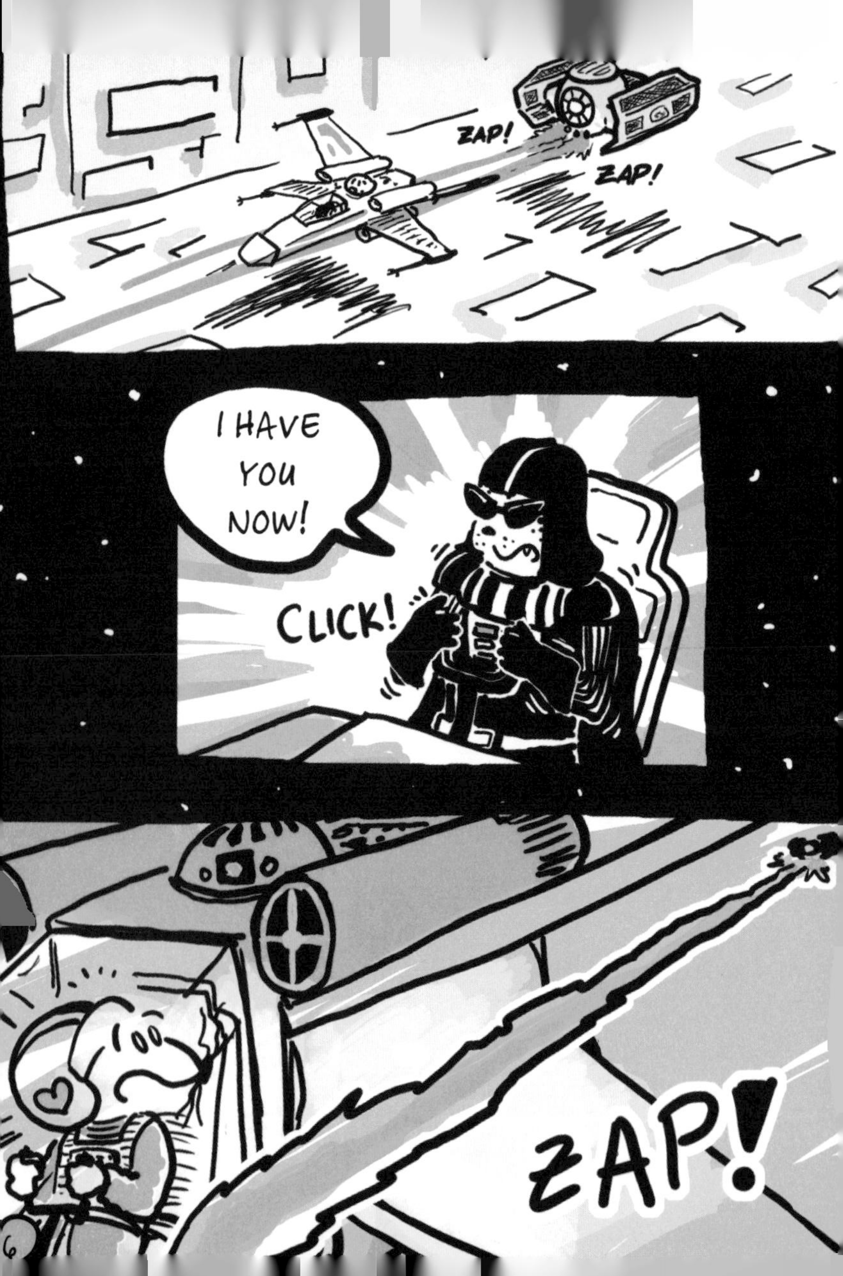
ZAP!
ZAP!
I HAVE YOU NOW!
CLICK!
ZAP!

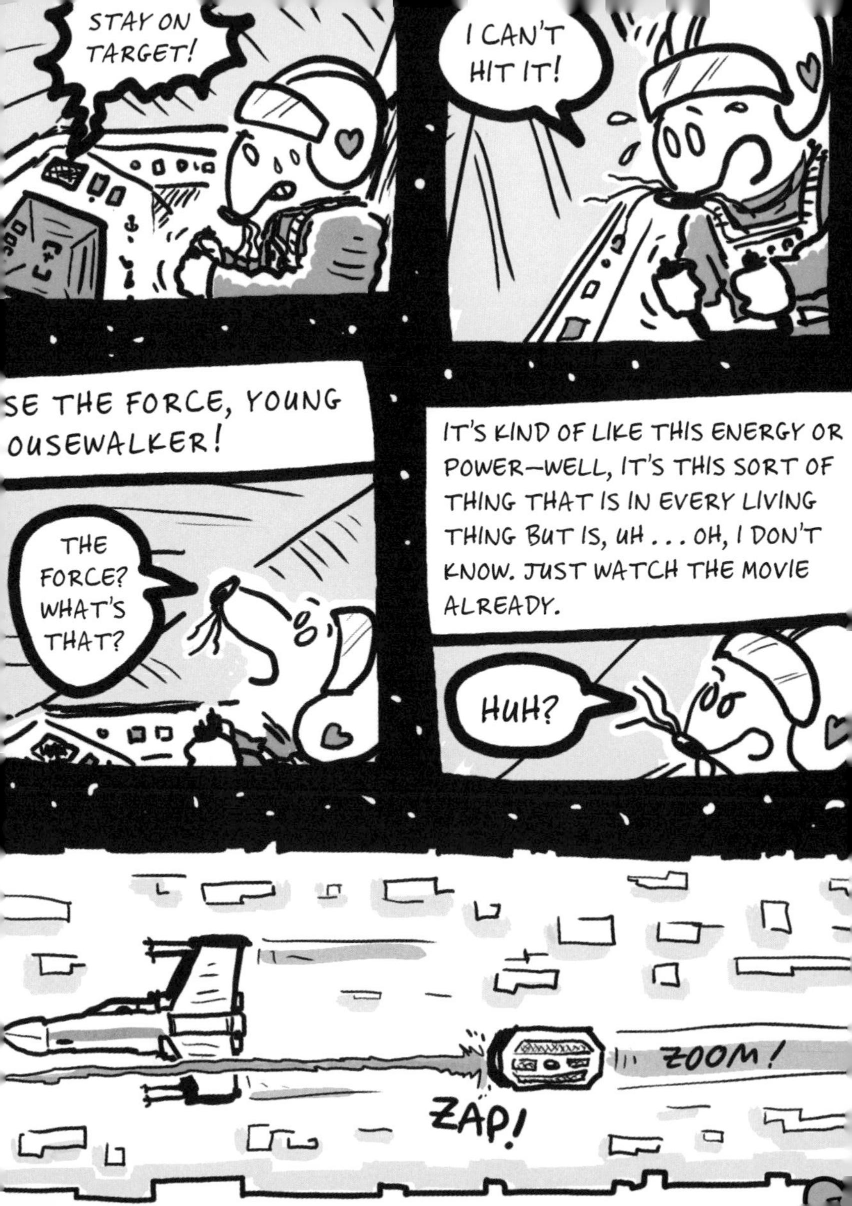
STAY ON TARGET!
I CAN'T HIT IT!
SE THE FORCE, YOUNG OUSEWALKER!
THE FORCE? WHAT'S THAT?
IT'S KIND OF LIKE THIS ENERGY OR POWER—WELL, IT'S THIS SORT OF THING THAT IS IN EVERY LIVING THING BUT IS, UH . . . OH, I DON'T KNOW. JUST WATCH THE MOVIE ALREADY.
HUH?
ZOOM!
ZAP!

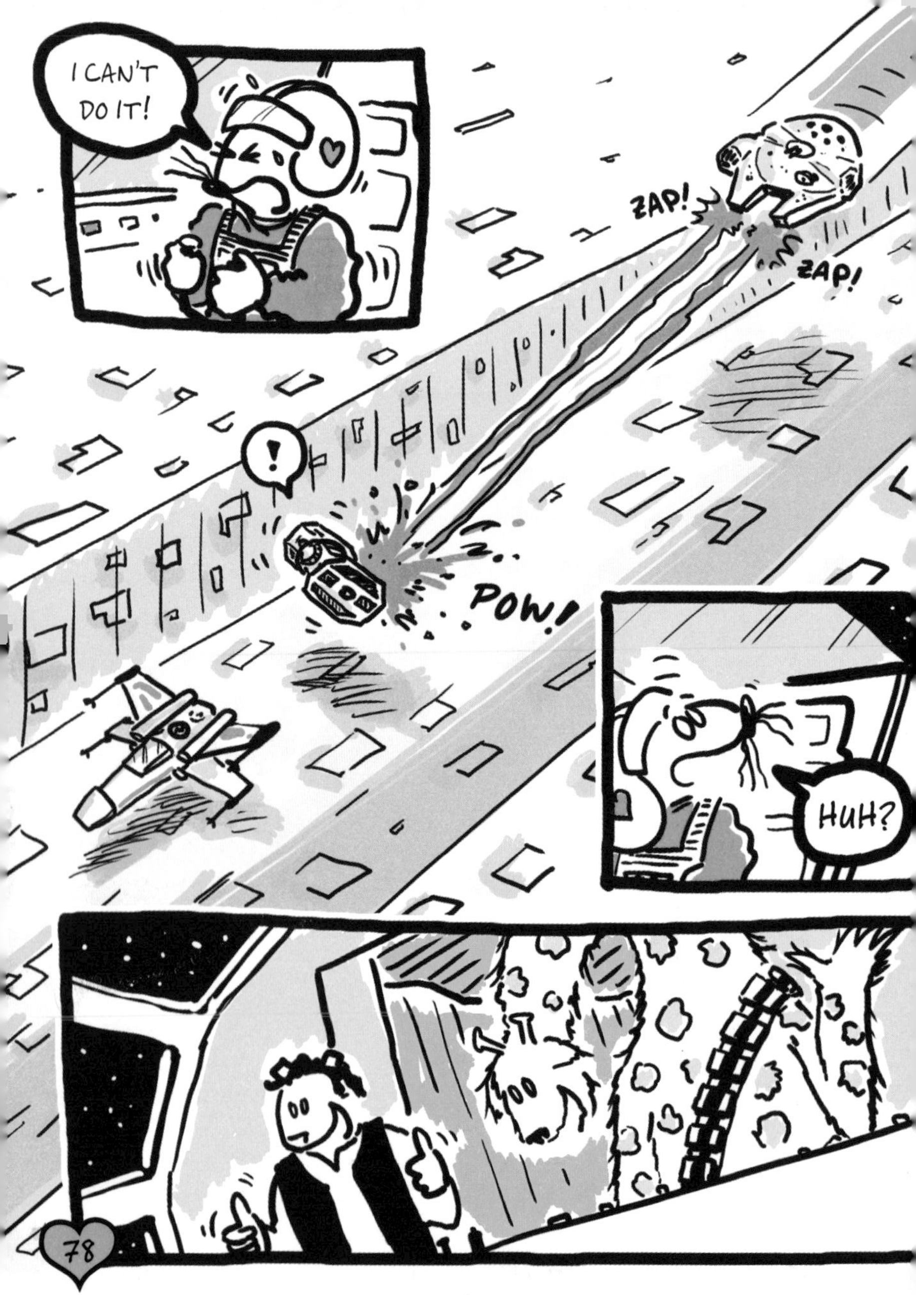

I CAN'T DO IT!
ZAP!
ZAP!
!
POW!
HUH?

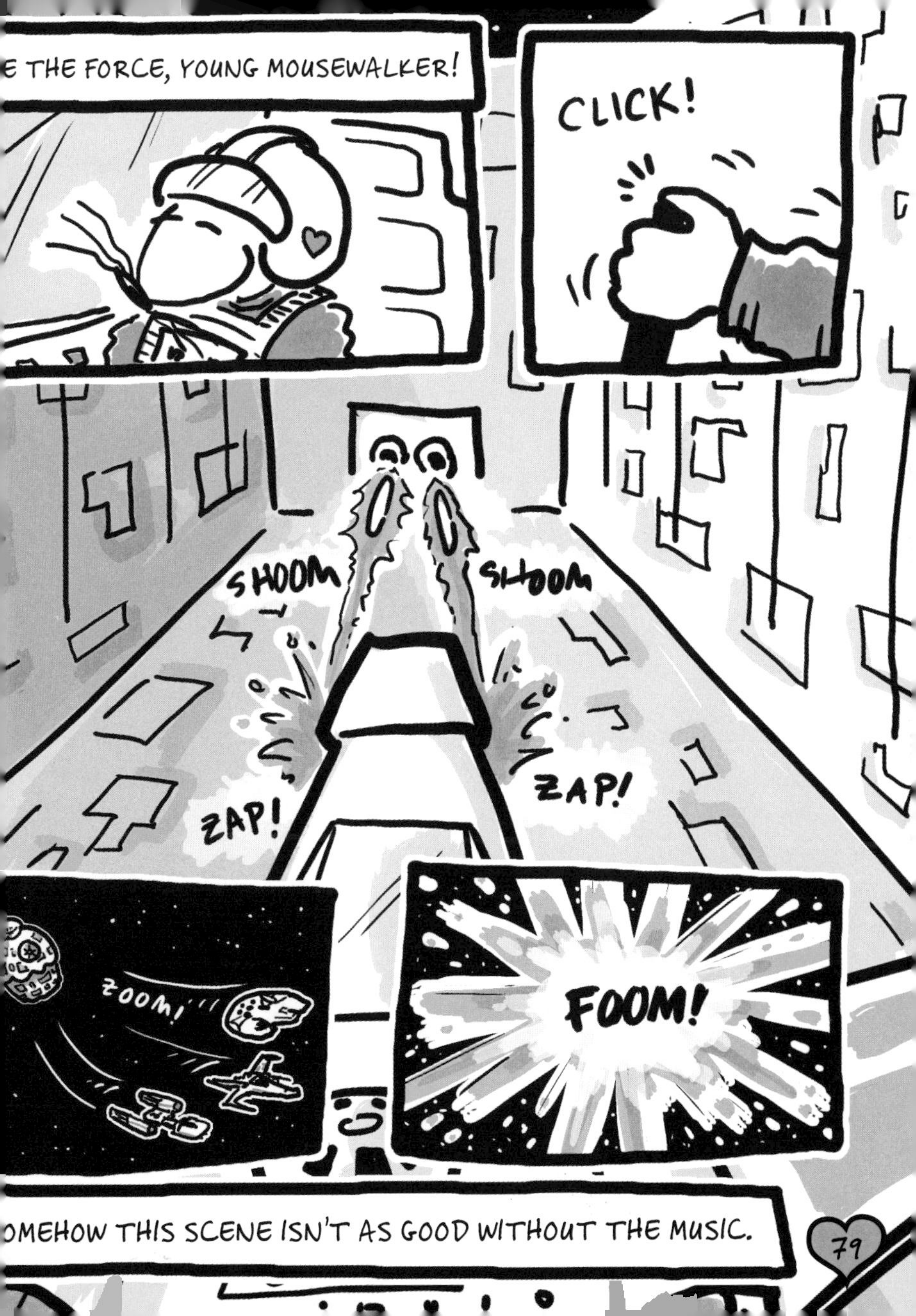
E THE FORCE, YOUNG MOUSEWALKER!
CLICK!
SHOOM
SHOOM
ZAP!
ZAP!
ZOOM!
FOOM!
OMEHOW THIS SCENE ISN'T AS GOOD WITHOUT THE MUSIC.

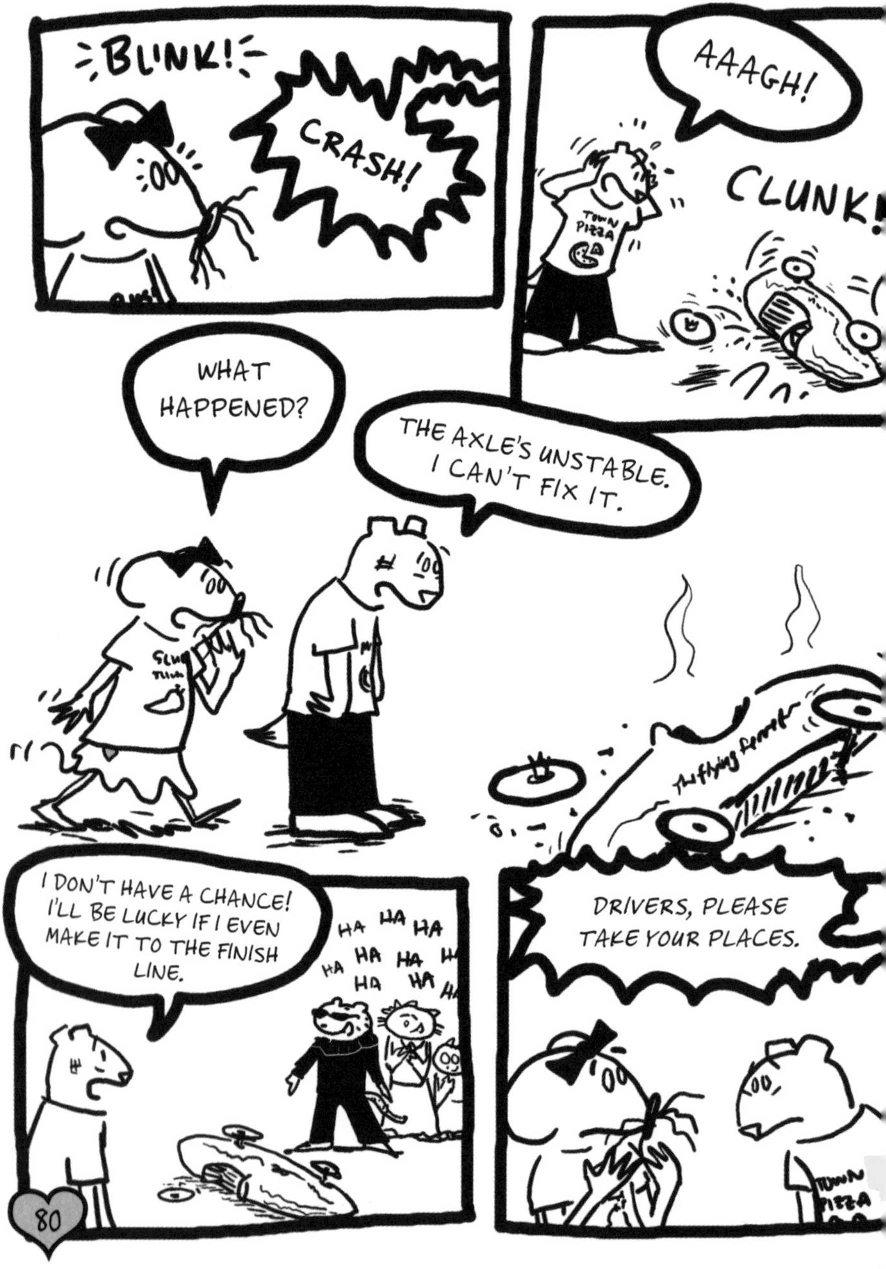
BLINK!
CRASH!
AAAGH!
CLUNK!
WHAT HAPPENED?
THE AXLE'S UNSTABLE. I CAN'T FIX IT.
I DON'T HAVE A CHANCE! I'LL BE LUCKY IF I EVEN MAKE IT TO THE FINISH LINE.
HA HA HA HA HA HA HA HA HA
DRIVERS, PLEASE TAKE YOUR PLACES.
TOWN PIZZA

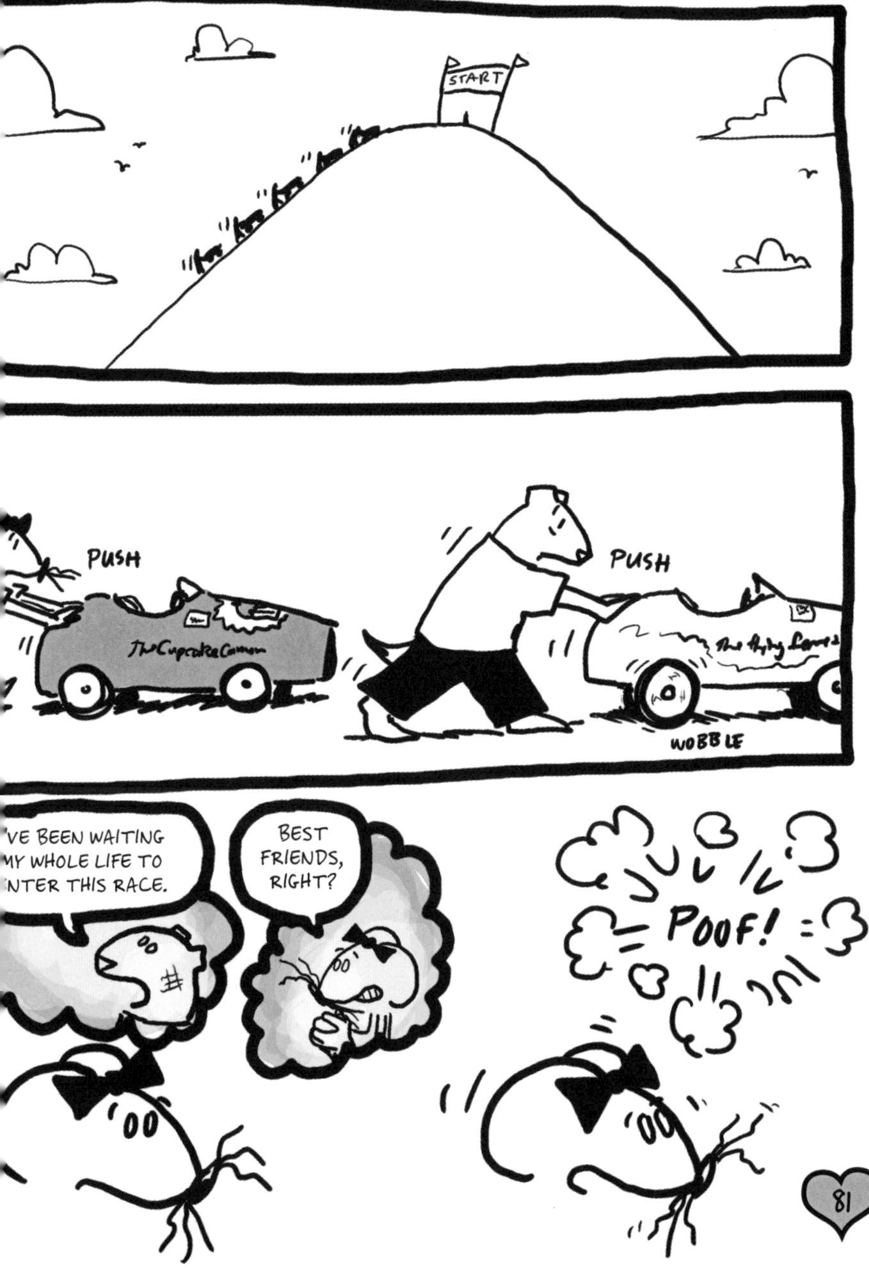
START
PUSH
The Cupcake Cannon
PUSH
WOBBLE
'VE BEEN WAITING MY WHOLE LIFE TO NTER THIS RACE.
BEST FRIENDS, RIGHT?
POOF!

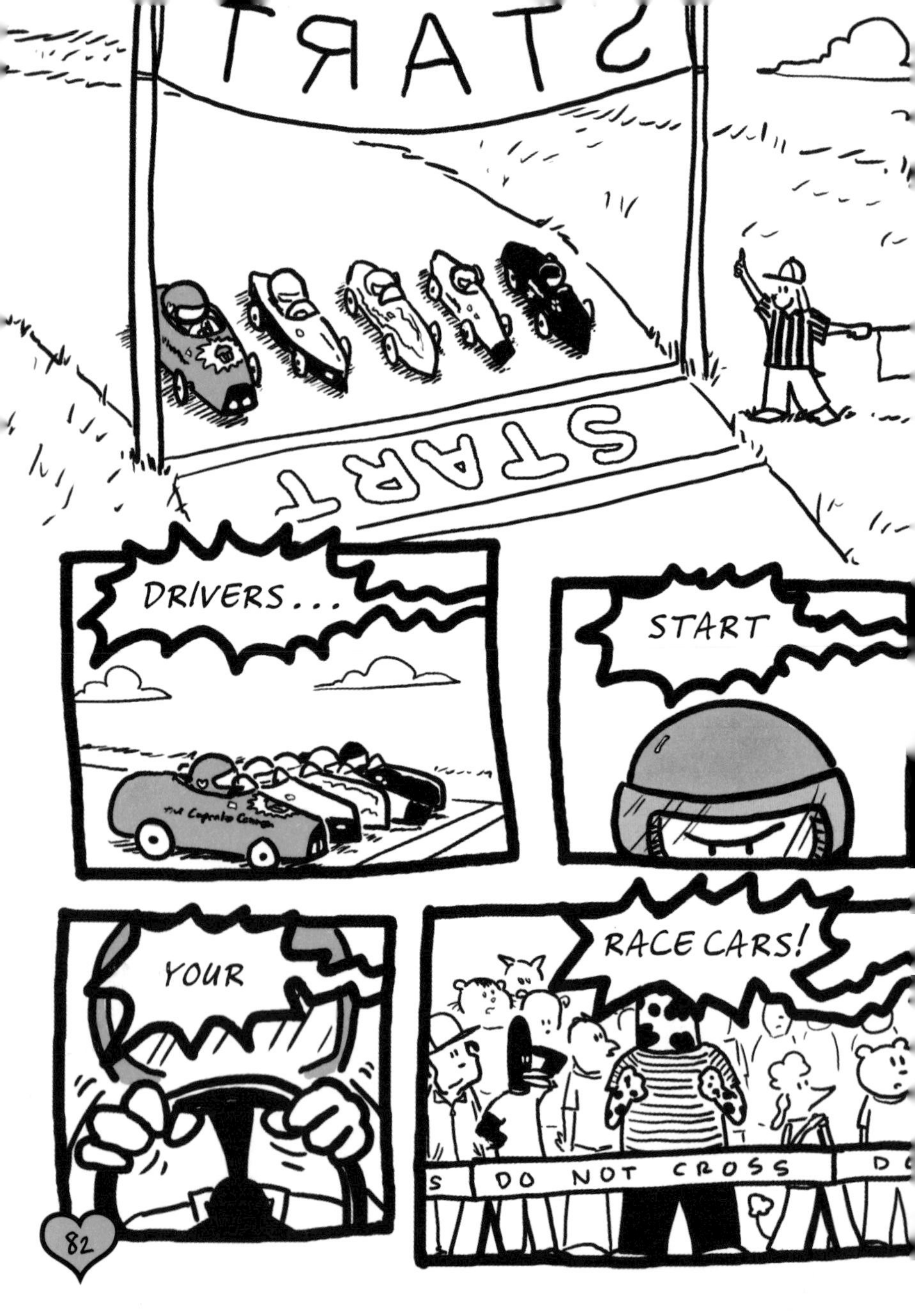
START
START
DRIVERS...
START
YOUR
RACE CARS!
DO NOT CROSS

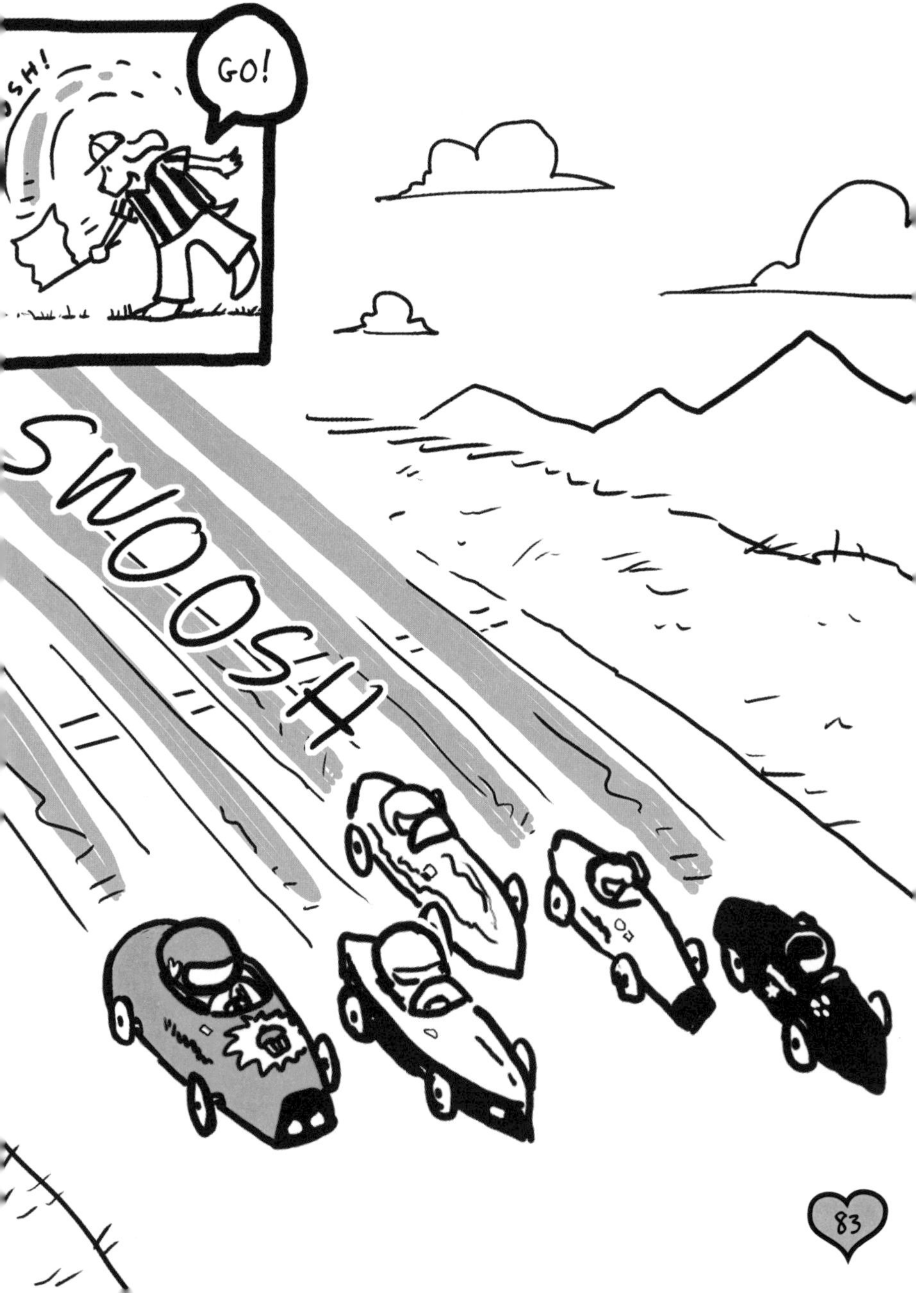

SH!
GO!
SWOOSH

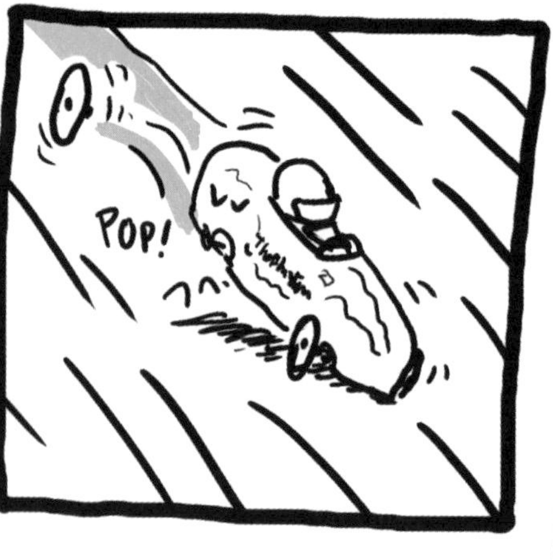
POP!

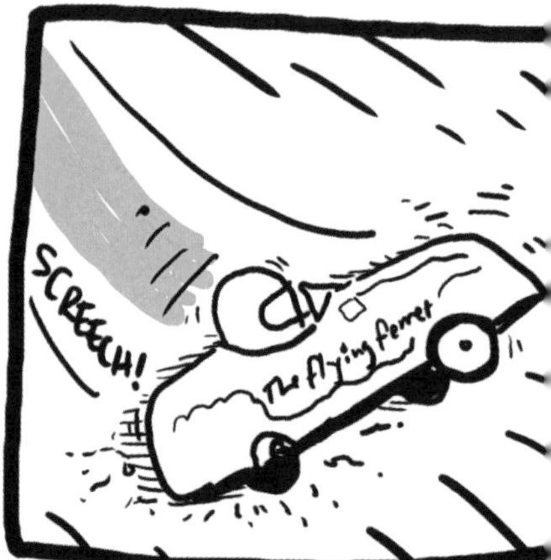
SCREECH!
The flying ferret

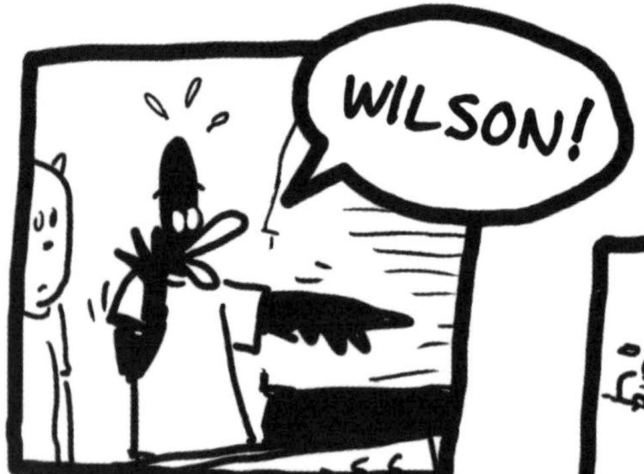
WILSON!

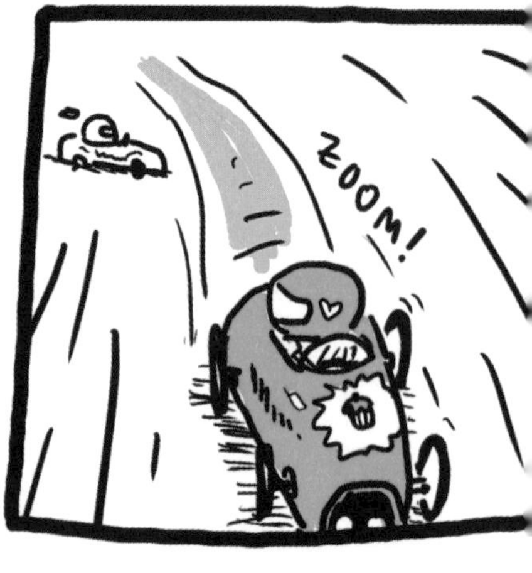
ZOOM!

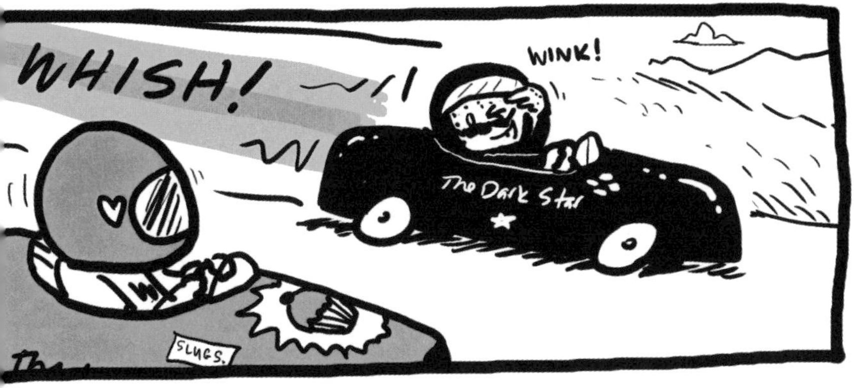
WHISH!
WINK!
The Dark Star
SLUGS.

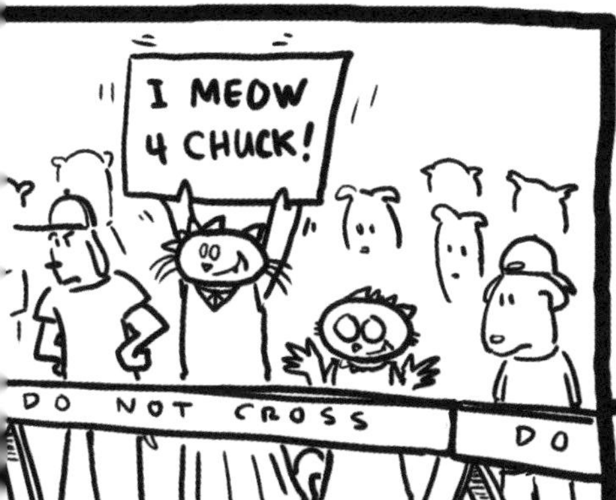
I MEOW 4 CHUCK!
DO NOT CROSS
DO

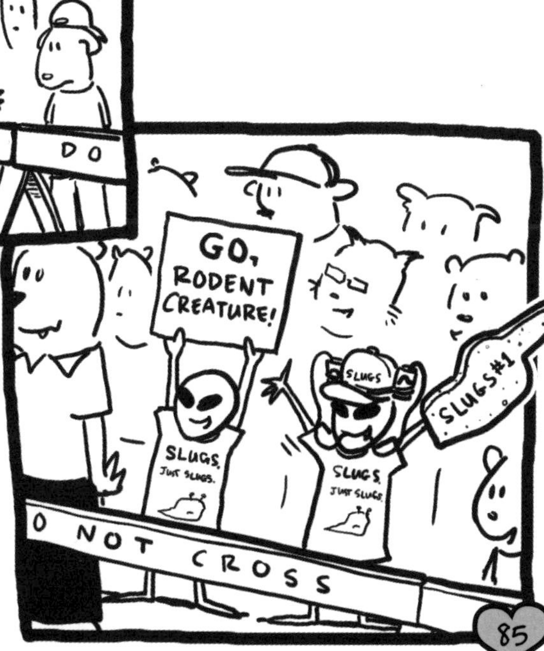
GO, RODENT CREATURE!
SLUGS
SLUGS #1
SLUGS. JUST SLUGS.
SLUGS. JUST SLUGS.
O NOT CROSS

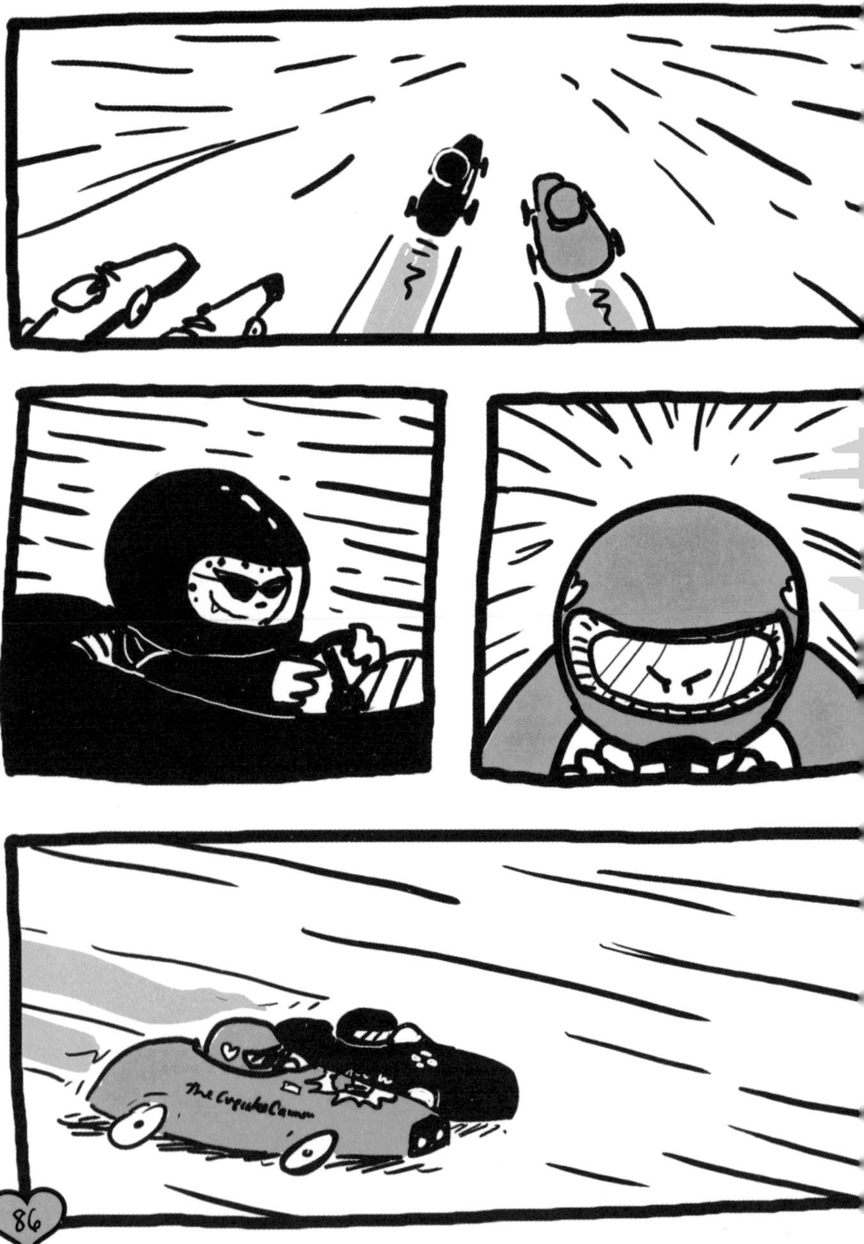

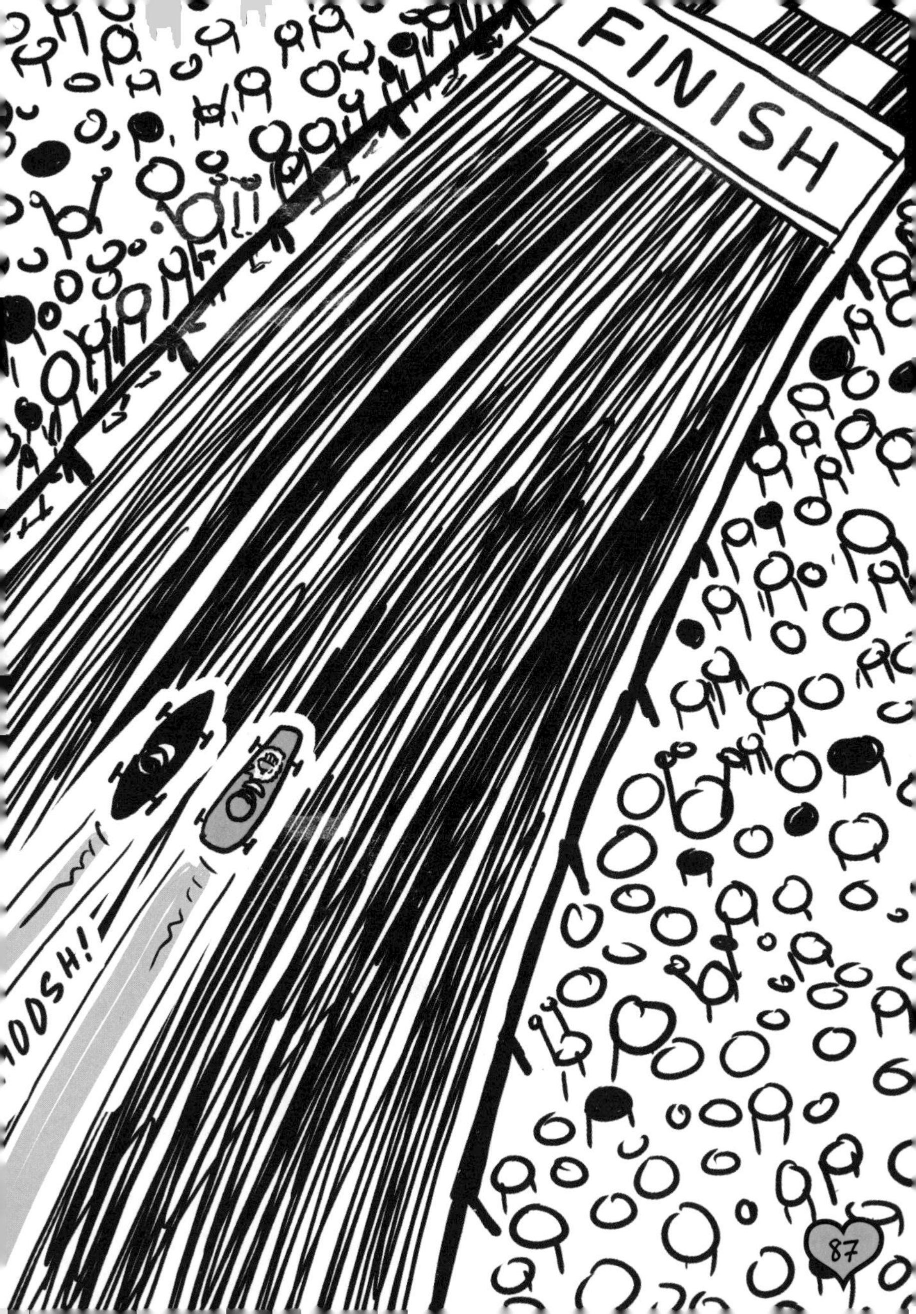
FINISH
OOSH!

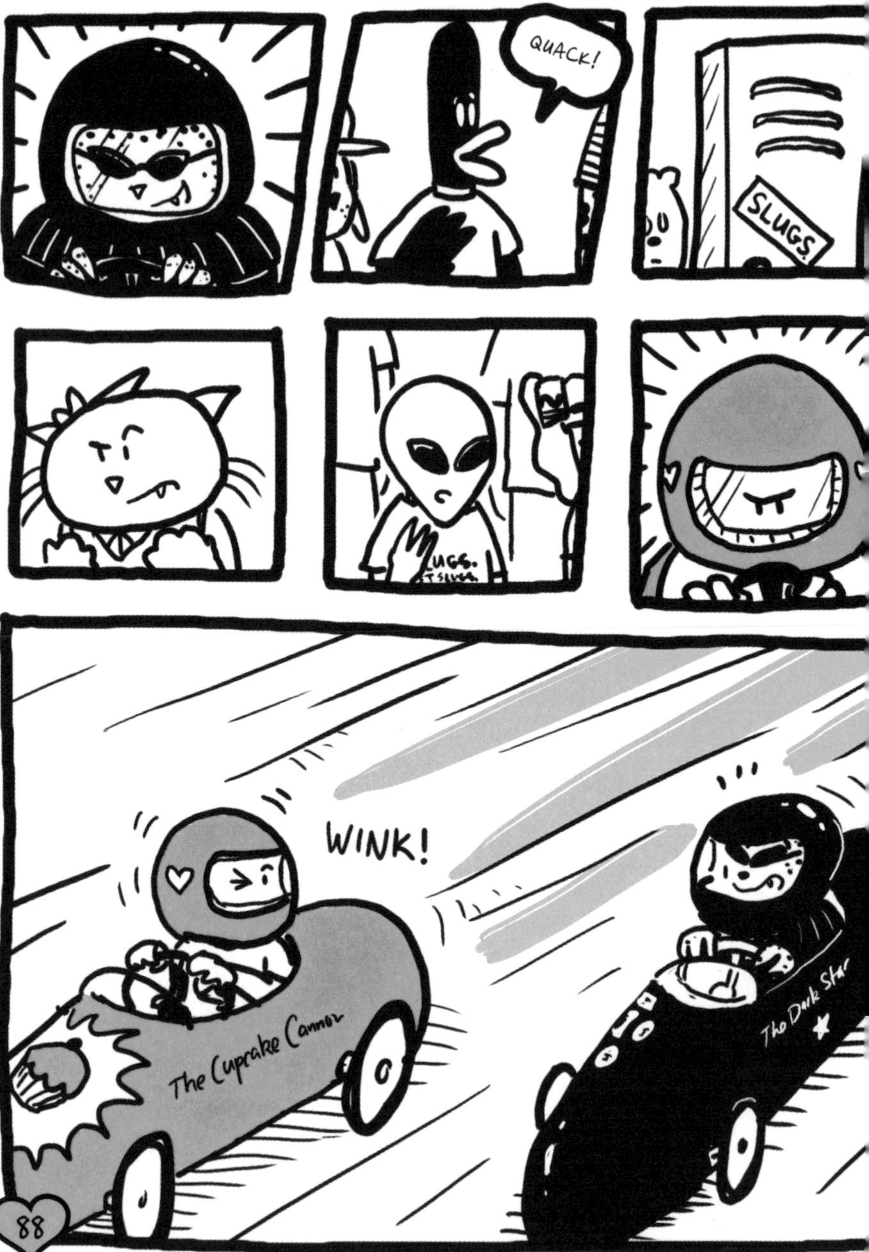
QUACK!
SLUGS
WINK!
The Cupcake Cannon
The Dark Star

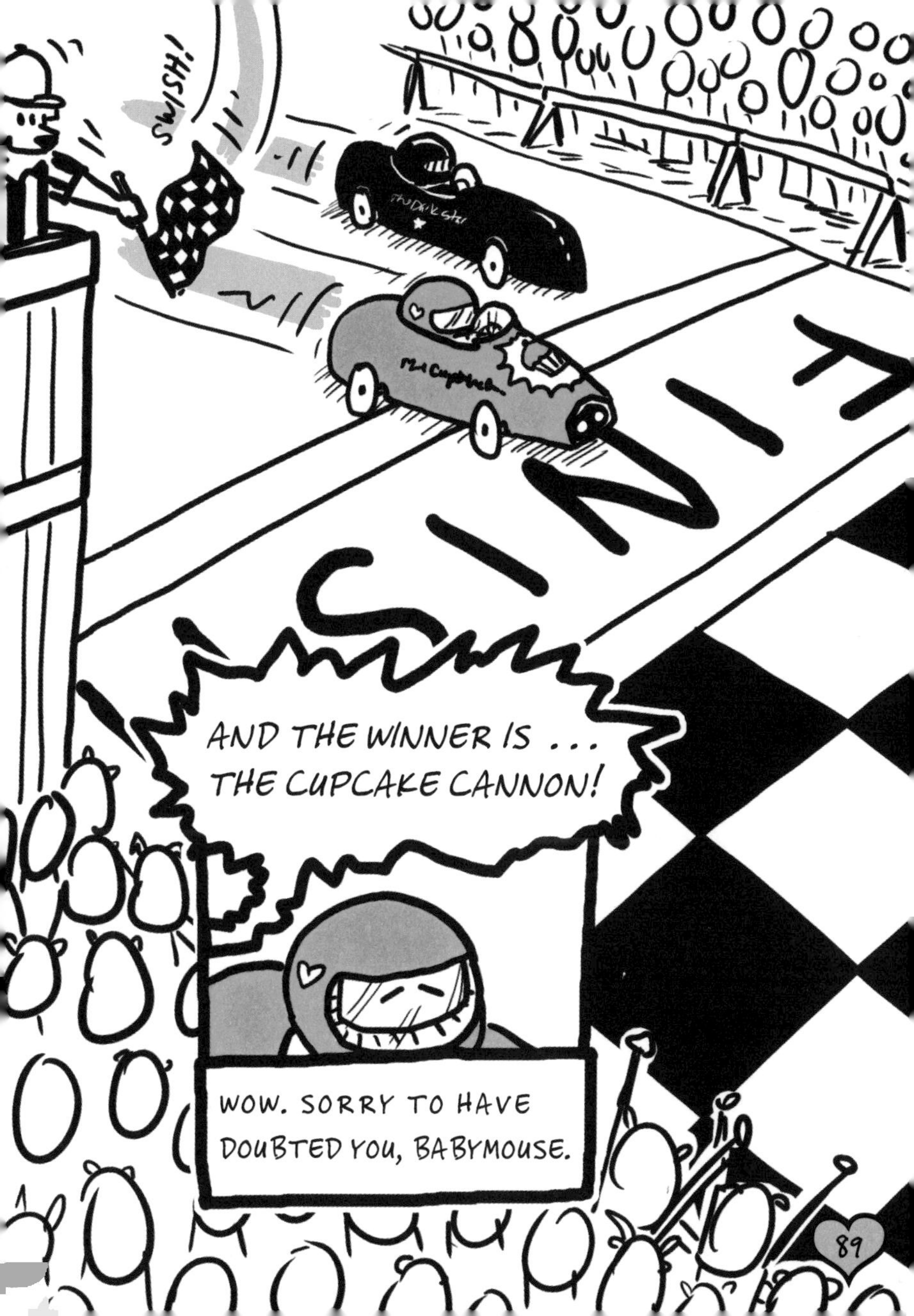
SWISH!
AND THE WINNER IS . . . THE CUPCAKE CANNON!
WOW. SORRY TO HAVE DOUBTED YOU, BABYMOUSE.

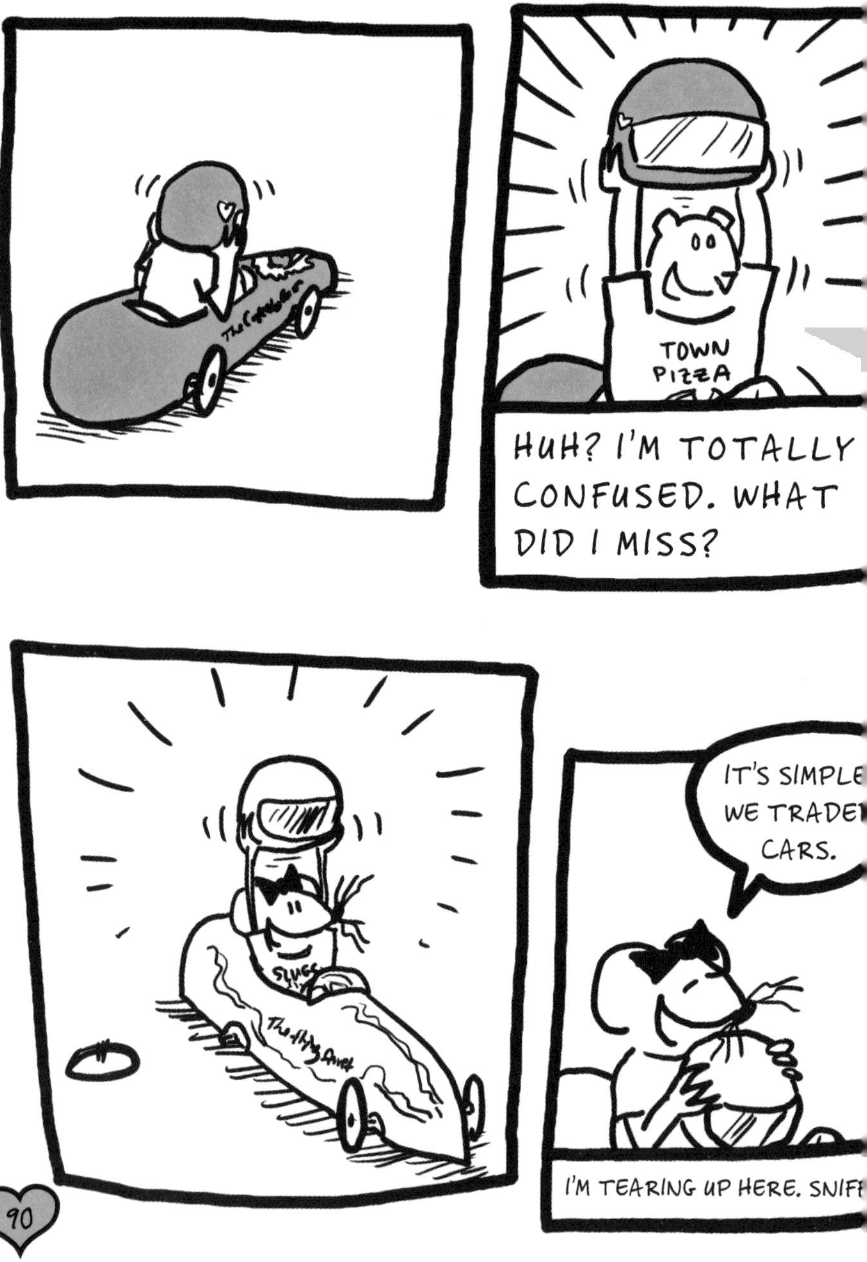
TOWN
PIZZA
HUH? I'M TOTALLY CONFUSED. WHAT DID I MISS?
IT'S SIMPLE WE TRADE CARS.
I'M TEARING UP HERE. SNIF

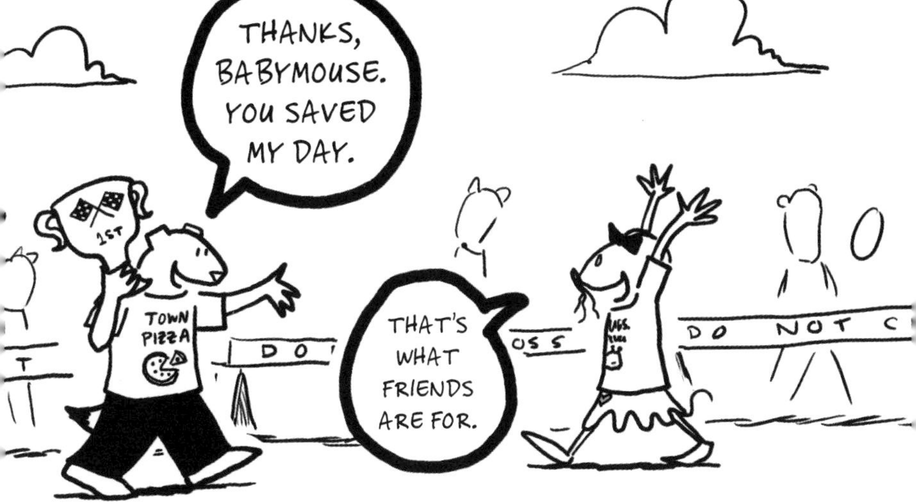
THANKS, BABYMOUSE. YOU SAVED MY DAY.
THAT'S WHAT FRIENDS ARE FOR.
TOWN PIZZA

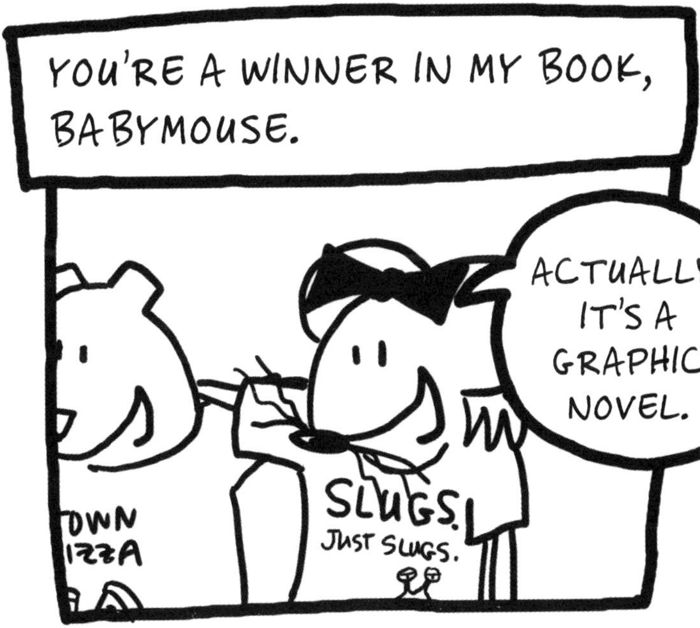
YOU'RE A WINNER IN MY BOOK, BABYMOUSE.
ACTUALLY, IT'S A GRAPHIC NOVEL.
SLUGS. JUST SLUGS.

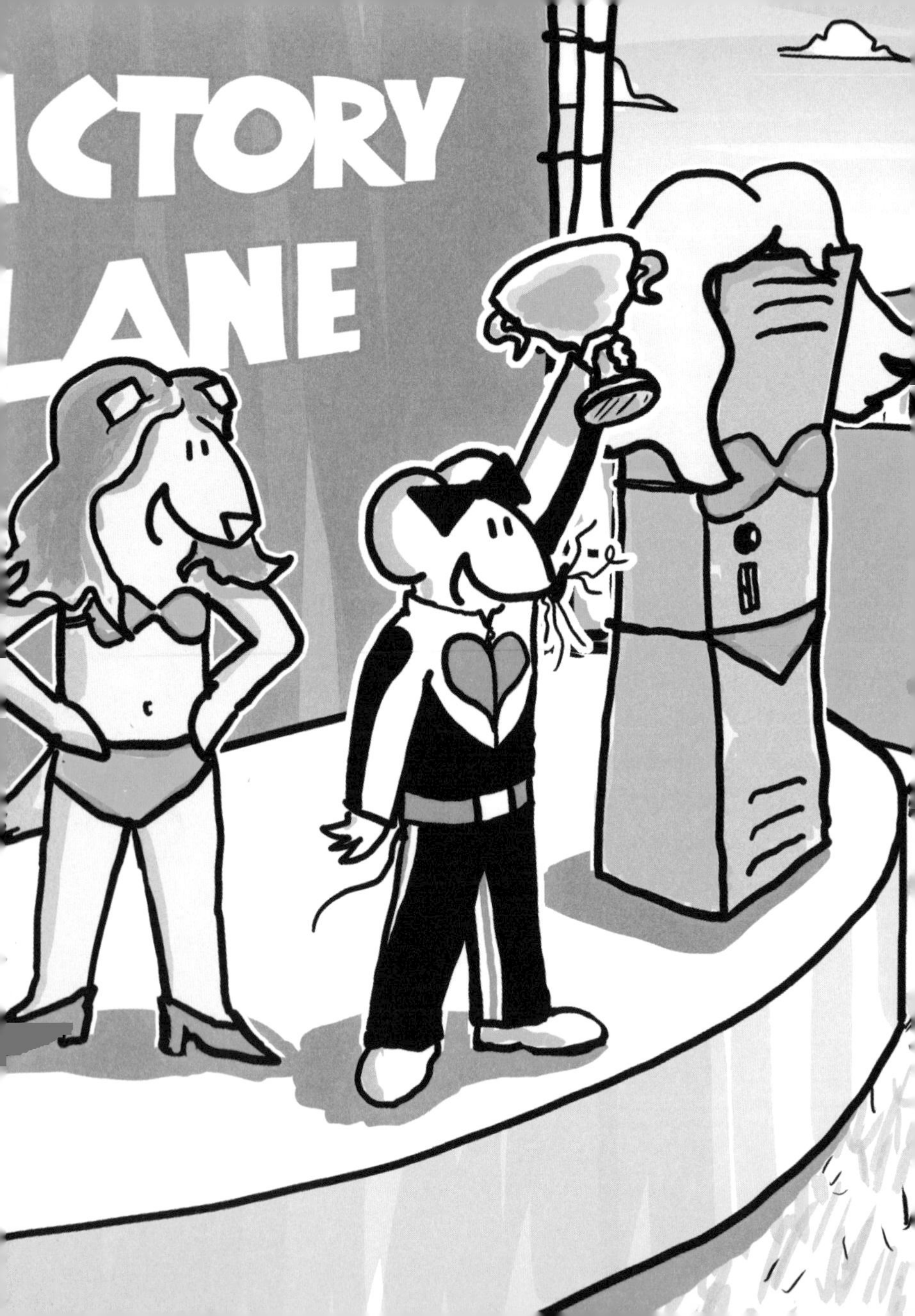
ICTORY
LANE

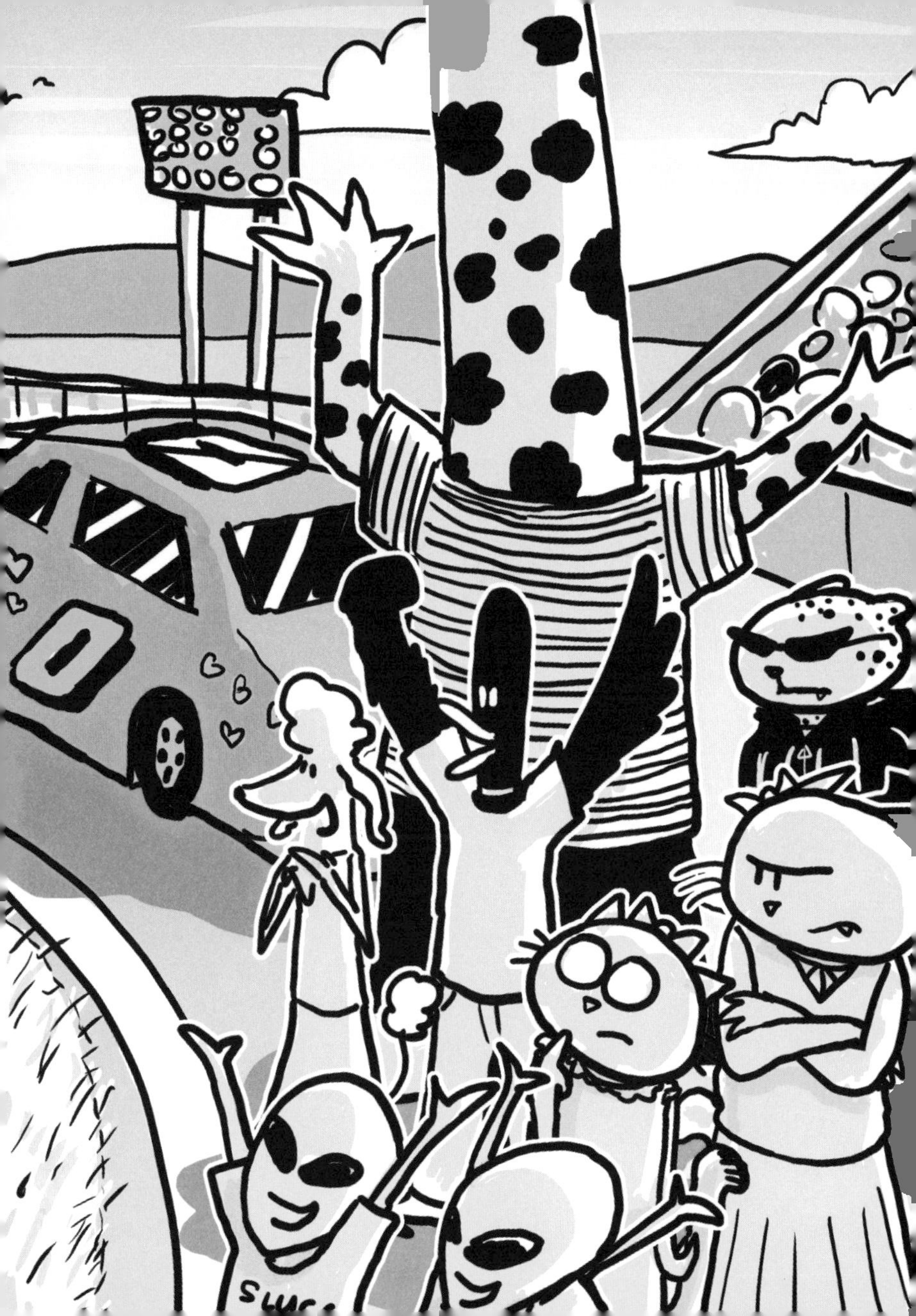

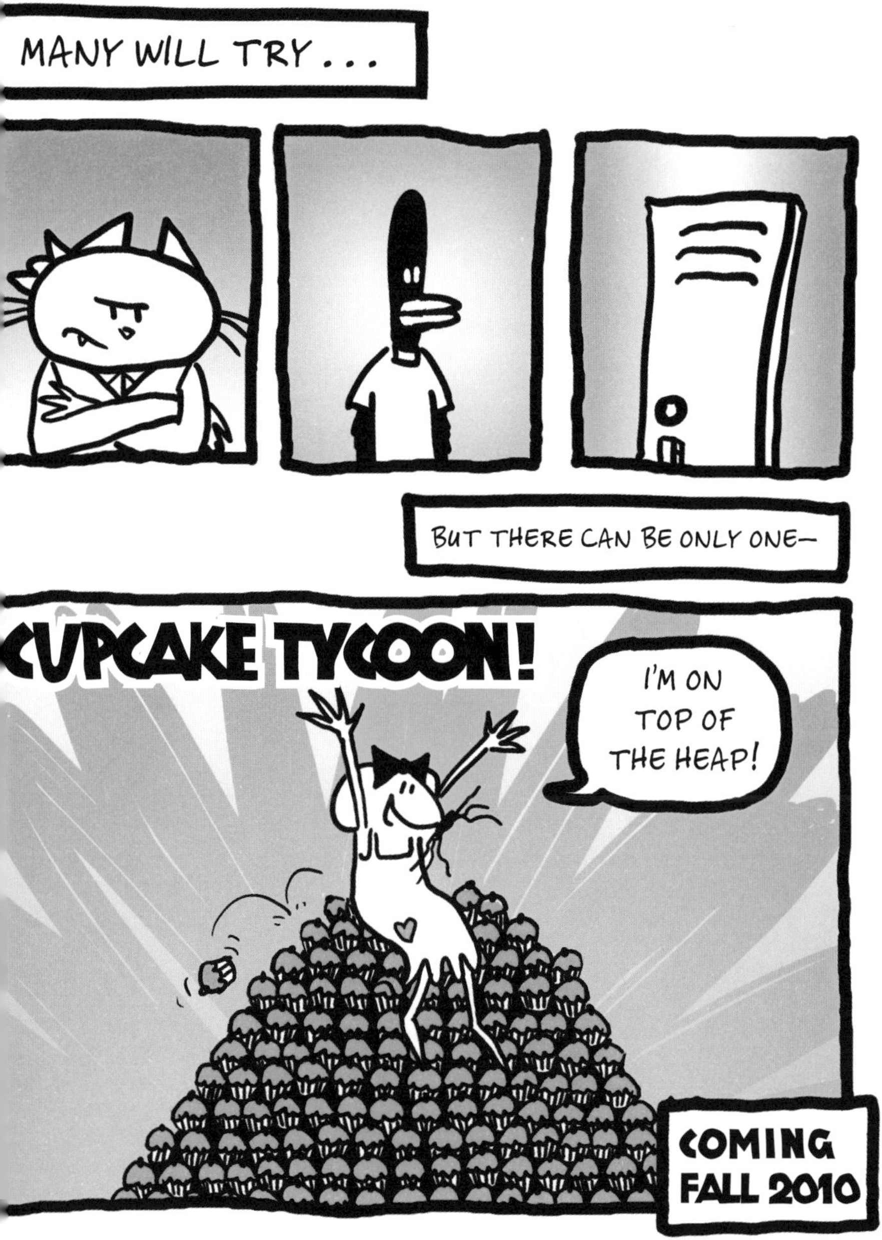
MANY WILL TRY . . .
BUT THERE CAN BE ONLY ONE—
CUPCAKE TYCOON!
I'M ON TOP OF THE HEAP!
COMING FALL 2010

BABYMOUSE BONUS!

• TIPS ON BEING A RACE CAR DRIVER •

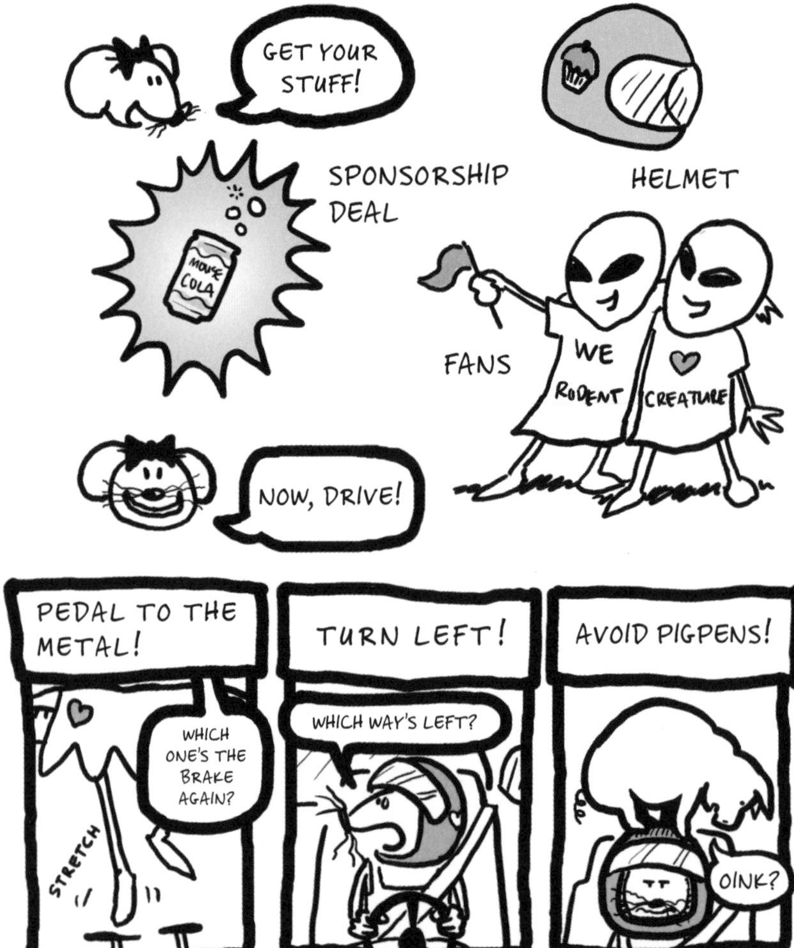

GET YOUR STUFF!
HELMET
SPONSORSHIP DEAL
MOUSE COLA
FANS
WE RODENT
CREATURE
NOW, DRIVE!
PEDAL TO THE METAL!
WHICH ONE'S THE BRAKE AGAIN?
STRETCH
TURN LEFT!
WHICH WAY'S LEFT?
AVOID PIGPENS!
OINK?